WRATH OF ABEL

SPECTRE OF CHAOS

SIMON HARRAK

ISBN: 978-0-6480128-5-6

SPECTRE OF CHAOS

1

LOYALTY WAS LIFE. Erik Burscheid had always believed that. What would the world look like without a commitment to one's family, to one's friends, to one's land? Without loyalty, there would be no civilisation. No progress. Empires grew because people did their duty. Those kids who treated their phones and even friends as disposable objects, they had no idea what an oath meant. You would get a blank stare if you asked them what long-service leave was. They owed their existence to the fact that their ancestors hung around. In the animal kingdom, staying together was the difference between survival and annihilation. Burscheid even stuck to his hairstyle, having had his ponytail since he was sixteen. He took pride in his consistency and dependability.

The League Of Reckoning was family, and Erik Burscheid would gladly sacrifice his life for it. He maintained loyalty at any cost, doing whatever the leadership asked of him. Pick-ups, drop-offs, mundane errands, breaking some bones here and there. Delivering a package or burying a body; it was all the same to him. It was all about loyalty.

He had just carried out his latest errand for The League, having dropped off the Abel kid to his apartment. As he left Abel's place, the weariness of the long drive back from Copenhagen had hit him like a sedative. He picked up a Currywurst with fries for lunch then headed to the Grand

Luxus to get some rest in his room. The search for street-side parking needed more time than usual, since the out-of-town soldiers bolstering Kalakia's fortress had taken most of the spots. At least Burscheid could sleep easy knowing they were out there.

Once he managed to find a spot at Zoologischer Garten, he crossed the intersection and made for the hotel. He passed several soldiers on the way, many of whom he knew well, but still did not acknowledge — official policy. At the entrance, however, he did pay attention to a bright green food truck selling hot dumplings. He gave it a long glance while continuing toward the revolving glass door. Then he stopped. He spun around and glared suspiciously at the man inside the van. There was something about him. He had a sweaty, chubby face with red cheeks and a downturned mouth. He was staring into thin air and tapping his fingers on the bench. *What's bothering you then?* Burscheid kept staring, analysing every feature of the man, bemused by his presence. Then Burscheid smiled. For all he knew, the guy's one-night-stand from a couple of months ago had just called and told him he had knocked her up. If that were the case, then he would need to consider sticking around for the kid to have any chance at life. No running away. Not like Burscheid's father had. Coward.

The fatigue was getting to Burscheid. He knew that because his mind was wandering. He had barely stopped in the few days since the attacks. The nap would do him good. He forgot about the sweaty-faced man and went through the revolving door. He was looking forward to that king-sized mattress, and figured he could even have a nip of whiskey before he dozed off.

2

The milk had coated her feet white. A thick pool of it flowed slowly outwards from the pot which had hit the floor with an ear-piercing clang. Her sharpened, disbelieving eyes remained on Kalakia as she studied his face, barely breathing, not daring to move.

Kalakia broke the stand-off by stepping around the mess and picking up the pot, placing it on the kitchen bench. He then lifted the tea towel from the cabinet handle and crouched down to begin dabbing the milk off his mother's feet. Before long he felt a hand on his shoulder. He froze, then stood up. With a gasp she lunged forward and wrapped her arms around him. He responded by placing a hand behind her head and pulling her firm, tiny body into his chest.

"You're here," she said, pulling back and placing a hand on his cheek. "My boy," she added, her eyes now softening and filling with tears.

Kalakia looked carefully at his mother. He had not seen her in over four decades. She was smaller than he remembered, and she had lost weight, especially around her face. She appeared weary, but her stare remained potent, seeping into him and flooding him with old emotions.

"Come," she said, placing a hand on his wrist. "Leave the mess."

She took off her shoes and placed them by the doorway before walking barefooted into the living room, where Kalakia followed and found her on the couch. He passed by her and ran his fingers along the old books on the shelf. The classics were still there, including Dostoyevsky and Tolstoy. Kant's 'Critique of Pure Reason' also caught his eye. He recalled how much of an insatiable reader his father had been.

"Sit, my boy," said his mother and patted an empty spot beside her.

Kalakia complied. *My boy*. He had not heard that phrase in a long time.

"I felt it was important to see you," he said as he sat. "Trouble is coming."

She nodded solemnly as though she understood everything.

"Trouble has always followed you, and you have always conquered it."

"This is different."

"I thought about you many times over the years," she said, ignoring his ominous statement.

"Did you?" he said.

"Of course."

"I assumed you would try to forget me," he said.

"Forget you?" she said with a headshake. "Nonsense. You are my son. I was angry at you, that is true. Angry at what you did to that boy, the path you took."

The image of Arman falling down the cliff shot up with a thump. Kalakia remembered how Arman's hair felt as he clutched it and mercilessly dragged the young boy to the edge and tossed him over. He heard Arman's dreadful scream echoing over the valley.

"I disappointed you," he replied.

"You did," she said. "And I have forgiven you. I did so long ago."

Kalakia recalled his mother's anguish when news came that her son had committed murder. She had wept, continuously shaking her head and repeatedly whispering 'no,' refusing to accept it, until his father led him out the door. She had been too weak to follow them, crippled by shock and grief. Her scream from inside the house had been the last thing Kalakia heard before his father forced him into the backseat of their car.

"Do you know why I forgave you?" she asked.

"No," said Kalakia.

"Because I finally understood something. You did not choose the path you took. Your future was already written."

Kalakia felt the fog of sorrow come over him. He knew what she meant. Sensing the shift, his mother reached over and placed her hand on his cheek as though he were still that boy.

"You carried the burden for all of us," she continued. "Your father was too distracted, your brother as well. For them, reputation was everything. They were not interested in the truth. It was too painful to face."

Kalakia listened carefully, mesmerised by his mother's insight.

"But you were different. You accepted who you were," said his mother. "My little warrior," she added with a tender smile.

Kalakia blinked and nodded.

"You have reflected on this for a long time," he said.

"I had a lot of time to think after your father died. Are you still angry with him for sending you away?"

Kalakia's jaw shut tight. He nodded.

"He also had no choice," she said.

"He only cared about what others thought of him."

"True, but it was more complicated than that. He loved you."

"Did he? After Kraas went away, he barely spoke to me. The whole town looked down on us, and he would have fallen to his knees for them to accept him. Even when Kraas joined the armed forces, they still mocked us. Nothing we did was going to wash away the shame of who we were. We remained gypsies to them. Uncultured and uncivilised. Filth, and nothing more."

"Your father could not help who he was. Just like you could not."

"I defended our honour. What did he do? He disowned me for it."

"He sent you away to protect you. They were going to kill you."

"You believe I could not have defended myself? He underestimated me, and worse still, he underestimated himself. He always did. Do you know what Arman said before I killed him? 'Your family are a pack of dogs, trying to walk on two feet like humans.' You do not reason with such people; you humble them with force. It was then I realised my father's way would not work. Men respect only strength and power."

"You've had the rage of a lion, ever since you were a little boy. And you've always been stubborn, even more than your father. Nobody could convince you to see things differently."

"Idealists. My father and Kraas."

Kalakia's mother gave a weary smile.

"I pray one day you'll understand," she said.

10

"I did not come to talk about them. I came to protect you from what is to come."

His mother's tenderness faded before his eyes, and her face turned hard. She lifted her chin and intensified her stare.

"Do you think I would need your help after all these years?" she said.

Kalakia smiled and shook his head.

"Every lion was birthed by a lioness," he said.

"And don't you forget it," she snapped back before standing up. "Will you stay for lunch?"

Kalakia checked the time.

"I will," he said.

"Good, I'll get started right away," she said before going into the kitchen.

Kalakia leaned back on the couch and gazed into space, thinking again about the day he murdered Arman. His father's furious response. The fistfight which almost broke out between him and his father. The frantic drive to the train station to escape Arman's family. The tight knot in his chest which he felt in exile every morning since that day.

Now Kraas was dead, and Kalakia's life was under threat. The League was at war. With mayhem all around, Kalakia sensed his mortality for the first time in decades. With it came an irresistible craving to return home and revisit his past. To see his mother, and make sure she remained out of Stirner's reach. The coming war would descend like the plague, and nothing would be the same once the dust settled. Above all, Kalakia had to admit; he came to visit because he craved the comfort that only home offered. He hoped it would inject him with the strength to face what was ahead.

He closed his eyes. The symphony of birds chirping came through from outside. He could hear his mother rattling around in the kitchen, just like when he was a boy. His father would be in his reading chair, Kraas would be out somewhere plotting his next scheme.

A knock on the door interrupted Kalakia's nostalgia. He tilted his head. *Francois.* He went over to the front door and opened it.

"Stirner's people made contact," said Francois immediately. "He wants to speak with you."

The pitch-black had swallowed them whole. Shirvan's erratic breathing followed Brunswick from behind, the resonance of their shuffling feet on the tunnel interior amplifying each step. Brunswick's stomach growled, while a sharp pain throbbed in her thigh. She knew where the tunnel led, but that barely made walking in total darkness any less unsettling.

It was six kilometres from the emergency facility to the tunnel opening. They would only know they had reached their destination when they saw the light coming through the cracks of the entrance. Until then, they would have to carry on through the abyss with barely a sense of time or space.

"How long do you think it's been?" whispered Shirvan from behind.

They had barely spoken since they left the emergency facility.

"An hour, I think," said Brunswick.

"I hope they're ok back there."

"They'll be fine," she snapped, wiping the sweat off her face.

Did he have to remind her? She had pushed the situation in the emergency facility to the back of her mind. The chaotic escape that led to the deaths of Aiko, Lena and Jonas had demoralised them. Especially Brunswick. Finding themselves in an even tighter space without food had tipped them over the edge. The firefight in the main facility had cut off the power. Everyone was hungry, exhausted and afraid. After the scuffle between Phil and Vitaly had broken out, Brunswick knew they had to act. She had deliberated for a long time before deciding that the secrecy of the Neutralaser project was no longer a priority. Something terrible had happened to Michael, Brunswick was sure of that, and that meant they would need to call someone else for help. She fired up the battery-operated satellite phone and made contact with the Inselheim Group. The Chief Security Officer Anke Müller called back and said that she had given a NATO unit the coordinates for the concealed tunnel exit. With a rough time window for extraction, Brunswick and Shirvan left immediately, terrified that The League Of Reckoning would figure out where they were.

Must be close now, thought Brunswick, realising she had been on autopilot. Shirvan had said nothing for a long time.

"Sorry," she whispered absentmindedly.

"What?" said Shirvan from behind.

"Sorry I snapped at you before," she said.

"Don't worry about it," he replied. "You're doing fine."

Bullshit. There was nothing 'fine' about losing three of their friends, she thought.

"I think we're close now," added Shirvan. "We have to be."

They proceeded in silence for a long time, before Brunswick saw a soft glow in the distance.

"There," she said.

The appearance of their goal injected Brunswick with a thrust of energy that carried her forward. The aches in her body dissolved. She picked up her speed, kicking a large rock and almost tumbling over. Shirvan's breathing rate increased behind her. The details and shape of the tunnel emerged, and patches of dirt and tiny pebbles on the floor appeared, along with the bare-concrete walls and ventilation system. Finally, they made it to the over-sized, hydraulic-powered steel loading cage. With Shirvan's big eyes looking at her, Brunswick stood panting under the dim moonlight coming through the cracks between the boulders used to camouflage the tunnel entrance above.

"We made it," said Shirvan. "God, let's not do that again."

Brunswick rubbed his arm then marched over to the control panel mounted on the side of the cage.

"I can't hear anything," said Shirvan.

Brunswick trained her ears to the surface. The rescue team was probably still hours away. That was not going to stop her from going up. She pushed the button, and a loud whirring noise came from beneath their feet, as the cage began rising upwards with enough force to lift the mammoth weight of steel and rocks.

At the top they were greeted by the moonlight. Brunswick walked out onto the dirt and raised her head to the sky before sucking in an enormous breath of freedom. She gave a sigh of relief and stretched her neck, savouring the moment.

Her ears went stiff. A rush of footsteps came towards her from behind. She turned and flinched hard. A group of eight commandos dressed in all-black approached with their rifles held across their chests. Brunswick automatically lifted her hands into the air.

"Put your arms down," said the group leader as the commandos surrounded Brunswick. "Nobody is going to hurt you if you cooperate."

Brunswick hesitated, then slowly lowered her arms. Shirvan came over to her side. The two of them gazed at the small fleet assembled at the tunnel entrance. It was clear that they were not NATO.

"Move it!" yelled the group leader to his soldiers.

The engines of four army transport trucks came on and revved up simultaneously. The fleet of vehicles formed a straight line, and one of the trucks drove onto the cage.

"Who are you?" said Brunswick when the first truck had descended into the tunnel.

The group leader gave her a brief stare before checking his watch then looking impatiently toward the horizon. Who was he worried might come, wondered Brunswick? She studied him and the rest of the team attentively but found no clue which gave away their affiliation. Suddenly she could not shake the feeling that she and her team were mere pawns in a high-level game of chess. It made her feel tiny and insignificant, creating a pounding in her ears and a pressure in her chest which threatened to burst wide open. She began shaking with rage. A cloud of dust from the tyres of the trucks then blew into her eyes, and she knew that she had been tipped over the edge.

3

The disturbing mix of emotions had Frederich levitating. He felt surprise at Ida's unexpected appearance, confusion at how Vidrik had been behaving. There was also the dark, familiar presence. Knowing that Vidrik had stalked and threatened Ida, as well as slaughtered her neighbour, Frederich was ready to rampage. Vidrik was a dead man, no buts about it. If only Frederich knew in Copenhagen what Ida had told him now. How could he have been so careless?

Standing in his living room with fists clenched, the chemical cocktail of surprise, confusion and fury exploded. He stepped forward and kicked the lamp over with a loud grunt, smashing it against the wall. Broken glass from the bulb crumbled to the ground. He grimaced from the sharp pain in his back where Vidrik's bullet had struck him and stood there with his chest heaving up and down.

"Frederich," said Ida sternly from the sofa. "Relax. Come sit here."

Frederich stared out of the window, dragged away by his thoughts. He had greatly underestimated Vidrik. He should have known. That demented look on his face was a dead giveaway. If Vidrik was crazy enough to follow Frederich to Copenhagen and try to kill him, he was capable of anything. He would go after Ida again. By letting Vidrik go, Frederich had placed Ida in terrible danger.

"Frederich," repeated Ida.

"Sorry," he said, exhaling slowly and moving away from the window. "I've put you at risk again." He sat down beside Ida, grasping his hands together and leaning forward.

"It's not your fault. I just don't understand what he wants from me. Can't you talk to Kalakia?"

"Vidrik's gone rogue. He went after me yesterday, but he got away. I… I let him escape."

"Do you know where he is?"

Frederich bit his lower lip and shook his head.

"Don't worry, we'll find him. I promise," he said.

"That's not why I came," said Ida. "I don't want anything to do with another killing. One time was enough."

"This guy is crazy, Ida. You won't be safe unless I stop him."

"Listen, you do what you like. If murdering people makes you happy, that's your problem. Just don't drag me into it. Spare me the macho bullshit. I came here for answers. I thought maybe this guy didn't get the message to leave me alone, that's all."

"He knew," said Frederich. "He didn't care."

"Ok. So that's the way it is."

The spectre of Vidrik hung thick in the air and sucked the life out of their conversation. So did the memory of Frederich and Ida's dreary last encounter at Lustgarten.

"I'm gonna go," said Ida.

She stood up and began walking out of the living room. Before Frederich knew it, the same intolerable ache hit him in the chest like the last time Ida walked away from him.

"Don't go," he said in a knee-jerk way.

Ida stopped before she got to the door and turned around. The dull pain spread from his chest to the rest of his body.

"Why not?" she asked.

Frederich shrugged.

"I don't know," he said. "Because I don't want you to. I want you to stay."

"Why?"

She was drawing him in again, trapping him with her questions. Only he was the one trying to keep her around. She stared expectantly at him.

"You're not going to make this easy for me, are you?" he said, hoping to buy more time.

Ida's cheeks turned red, and she scowled, ready to spit fire at him. He had nowhere to hide. *Tell her.*

"Look," he said. "I know you're angry. I went behind your back last time. I lied to you. I shut you out. I thought I was protecting you, but all I did was hurt you and put you at risk. Now I've done it again. I'm angry enough at myself. I can't take you being angry on top of that. Just let me help fix this. Please. If something happened to you…"

He felt hot everywhere, picturing Vidrik lurking over Ida with his deranged intentions. Ida's eyes were unflinching, trained directly at him like laser rays. She appeared to be thinking, contemplating the best way to tell him how stupid and inconsiderate he was.

"I promised myself that whatever happened, I was never going to let anyone take advantage of me again," she said. "No more shutting me out. If I see you holding back, I'm gone. Ok? I can take care of myself."

"Ok," said Frederich.

Ida nodded while maintaining a sharp expression which held Frederich in place like a misbehaving little boy caught in the act.

"So aren't you going to offer me a drink?" she asked suddenly, lifting her eyebrows.

Kalakia knew Stirner would be unable to resist. His mother was chopping the onions when he went into the kitchen to tell her. There was a brief moment of hesitation; a silent, reluctant acknowledgement that he was leaving too soon. They had barely begun to bridge the gap caused by the last forty years. She froze, the knife still in her hand, then nodded solemnly.

He emerged from the house and his sharpness of mind returned as the breeze hit his face. It brought with it the real world, where Kalakia was the most feared man on the planet. Inside he had merely been his mother's son. Her *boy*.

A group of ten soldiers stayed back to guard the road leading into Kalakia's hometown. The rest of the fleet drove over an hour away into the mountains as a security precaution before Francois dialled the connection provided by Stirner's people. He handed the phone to Kalakia. The call rang for almost a minute as Kalakia stood by. A childish power play, he noted. Finally, there was an answer.

The line remained silent for some time — another ploy.

"I do not blame you for not knowing what to say," said Kalakia. "Worry not, old friend. Your cowardice has spoken clearly."

Stirner let out a throaty grunt.

"*Old friend*," he said. "Consider it a favour between friends that I even made the call. I was going to finish you off without saying a word."

"It is far too late for courtesy. You are a traitor. That is how you will be remembered. The world will voice its disgust about what you have done, and then it will forget you."

"I have other plans for my legacy," said Stirner.

"You lack honour, and you lack imagination. Plan all you wish. The result will be the same."

"Say what you want. Just know, your tyrannical reign is over. A new order is emerging."

"You bore me, Stirner," said Kalakia. "Does this conversation have a purpose?"

"You won't be bored for long, don't worry," replied Stirner. "Oh, I have waited for this. It wasn't easy putting up with a pompous bastard like you. But that is what I do. I wait. And now, it's time. Your soldiers are ambitious people, and they are intelligent enough to see the truth. I can offer them *real* power. Your model is outdated. They're going to leave you in droves and come to me. By the way, Matthias Vidrik says hello."

Kalakia went quiet, giving Stirner all the space he needed to boast and run his mouth. Already Stirner had revealed a part of his strategy to target League soldiers for defection. Stirner was hinting at a war of ideologies. Kalakia maintained his silence.

"Ha!" said Stirner. "For once the great Kalakia is speechless. You know, you spent so much time focused on the illuminated spaces that you forgot to look in the shadows. You forgot the place that raised you. Sure, the governments and the elite feared you, but there was another group who truly despised you. How long did you expect them to tolerate all of this? Their retribution is coming."

Kalakia could sense Stirner's arrogance growing by the minute, morphing into hubris.

21

"One last thing," said Stirner. "Why did you send your men to my home? What did you hope to achieve by destroying it? Did you think I would be so stupid as to leave my family exposed?"

"We will meet again soon," said Kalakia and prepared to hang up.

"You burnt down my home," cut in Stirner. "Allow me to return the favour. Goodbye, 'old friend.'"

Stirner ended the call.

Burscheid assumed he was still wired from the drive. After twenty frustrating minutes he had found no way of relaxing, let alone falling asleep. The bed beneath him was the perfect blend of firm and soft, so that was not the problem. The whiskey had done little to ease his nerves. He had once heard on the radio while driving that counting backwards from one thousand would help him sleep. That had done nothing for him either. After a while he sat up and supported his back with the pillow. He found himself thinking about the man from the food truck. That chubby-faced ball of sweat looked like he had bottomed-out in life. He might have otherwise made it as an enforcer with The League. He had an intimidating look. He had the size. What was he doing serving dumplings from a food truck? Then Burscheid's eyes widened. *The truck.* It was taking up a large portion of the sidewalk and posing an unwelcome obstruction for the passers-by. No one in their right mind would allow it in such a high-traffic area. Without warning, the unease that had kept Burscheid awake emerged through the fog of fatigue, bringing with it a message of doom that sent tremors down Burscheid's spine.

He bounced off the bed and quickly put on his shirt. He ignored his socks and tossed his shoes on before rushing out, not bothering with the laces. Outside he slapped the elevator button multiple times. After some seconds, he grunted and took the emergency stairs instead, shuffling down the steps as quickly as possible and emerging in the lobby. The urgency overtook him, and he broke out into a jog. The front revolving door had people in it. He took the side door instead. Upon exiting he halted suddenly. The food truck was empty. In front of it were two teenagers, a boy and a girl with hole-riddled jeans and t-shirts. The boy was holding a dumpling while staring in confusion at the street. Burscheid followed his gaze and saw the chubby-faced man getting into a black Audi sedan.

"Why did he just leave like that?" said the boy to his friend in German.

A sharp pain shot through Burscheid's chest like a bullet had struck him. His legs began moving by themselves.

"Everyone move!" he screamed while swinging his arms frantically to the side. "Get away from the truck!"

He hugged the two teenagers as he approached and forced them along with him to the side. The boy holding the dumpling yelled out as his food flew out of his hand. Then the ground shook beneath their feet, the explosion scorching Burscheid from behind while lifting the three of them into the air.

Frederich flinched from the thunderous boom. Hot tea spilt on Ida's hand and onto the carpet as she almost lost her grip. The two of them lifted their heads simultaneously and looked at each other with worried expressions as aftershocks continued to rumble in the distance.

"What was that?" said Ida.

She leaned over and placed the cup on the table. Frederich went to the window but saw nothing when he looked out, only a clear sky. The two of them instinctively made for the door. They barrelled through the hallway and left the apartment, leaving the front door open, and quickly descended the stairs before going out to the front of the building and onto the street. There was a large plume of smoke rising in the air from the direction of Zoologischer Garten. People stood disoriented on the sidewalk sharing concerned expressions. Frederich did not doubt that The League was involved. He would need a closer look.

Ida was gazing up awe-struck at the smoke with her lips parted. She then lowered her head and turned toward Frederich with a dazed expression.

"Go inside, Ida," said Frederich.

In response her face hardened and she flared out her nostrils. Frederich got the message immediately. He nodded, and together they began running toward the source of the smoke. They reached the intersection of Kantstrasse where the traffic was at a stand-still. There were frightened faces everywhere. Frederich and Ida turned and sprinted in the direction of Zoologischer Garten. They ran the next few hundred metres against a stampede of terrified people. Eventually they reached Zoologischer Garten, where ambulance sirens, police sirens and pandemonium met them. They took a moment to catch their breath then worked their way around the crowd to the Grand Luxus hotel. It was barely recognisable, the explosion and resulting chaos having redrawn the entire area. Half of the facade was missing, and there was a large crater in the street. People lay screaming, bloodied, covered in dust, with ambulance personnel attending to them. The police were creating a security barrier around the scene, urging bystanders to leave the area. Frederich squinted and looked into the distance. Was it? Yes, it had to be. He recognised the ponytail and pale skin. It was Erik, hunched over on the ground. A medic approached but Erik waved him off. After multiple attempts, the well-meaning samaritan finally gave up and moved on to check on other people.

The screams were merciless. Frederich felt his insides being set ablaze by the piercing shrieks of agony before a deathly chill descended and made him completely numb. He turned toward Ida. Tears were streaming down her face as she took in the scene, her body shaking and teeth chattering. She searched for Frederich's hand without averting her eyes and found it, wrapping her fingers around his and grasping tightly. Frederich could feel her absorbing every ounce of the suffering around them, taking it into her embrace while buckling under the weight. Somehow she held on, gripping Frederich's hand tighter when the pressure threatened to overwhelm her, her unflinching gaze remaining on the senseless destruction that had hit the city.

4

Frederich arrived at Berlin-Wannsee station early in the afternoon after a thirty-minute train ride. He exited the station building then carefully re-checked the pinned location on his smartphone as people walked around him toward the street. He was still perplexed by the directions Intel had given him, which included a set of obscure coordinates accompanied by 'go there and wait for instructions.' They had not specified a time, so he decided on going before dark, and with Erik out of action, the train seemed like a good plan B.

The map showed Wannsee to be tucked in the south-west of Berlin, surrounded by lakes and an expansive forest. Marked on the screen were castles, villas and sailing clubs. The town itself was wedged between greenery on one side and water on the other. After the mayhem in Zoologischer Garten, the calming effect was instant. Frederich felt himself return to his body. Tingles ran over his skin and washed away his agitation. He sucked in the fresh air and absorbed the feel of the forest. The place reminded him of home. If Kraas were alive and came to visit Berlin, Frederich knew the first place he would have taken his father, who loathed cities.

Enough reminiscing. It would be dark soon. He cut through the town and went into the forest, following the footpath as far as possible. Another look at the map showed the coordinates to be deep in the area shaded dark green. He checked around to make sure he was alone then melted into the trees, travelling a couple of hundred feet through thick shrubs. Once the map showed he had reached the coordinates, he stopped and looked around. He hoped the satellite signal was accurate. The only possible place to go next was a small opening between the trees to his right. He waited a while then trampled in that direction through the bushes, hoping he would find the next clue. He got one better, when a pale, nervous-looking young man stood waiting for him. The kid's eyes seemed way too alert, and he looked malnourished. His black jumper sat loosely over his bony body, and he had on a pair of light blue jeans and old, torn-up sneakers.

"Come," he said as Frederich approached.

He turned and led Frederich out of the opening, through more thick bushes, until the overgrowth abruptly ended, revealing a well-concealed bunker entrance below eye level. The paved path was covered with scattered dirt and weeds while dipping sharply and leading toward a wide concrete entryway. At the top were three security cameras pointed in multiple directions, and there was a 'Restricted Area' sign on the sidewall. The concentration of surrounding trees and shrubs did an effective job of keeping the light out. Deep inside it was completely dark.

"In there," said the kid, pointing into the shadows.

Frederich gave him a courteous nod. He took a glance backwards as he began walking in, feeling the downhill pressure on his heels, but the gaunt young man had already disappeared. While Frederich walked with his head still turned, he collided into something hard and unyielding. It was like hitting a wall, sending shockwaves through his face and neck and bowling him over.

"You right there, Abel?"

Frederich quickly reoriented himself and found himself face to face with an unimpressed looking Scheffler, standing with his typical man-mountain stance, legs wide apart and shoulders back. The singlet was gone, replaced by a black, buttonless shirt similar to what Kalakia wore. Scheffler was also clean-shaven and had his hair brushed neatly to the side.

"Scheffler?" said Frederich.

"No, it's Winston Churchill. Did you damage your brain? You need to watch where you're walking."

"No, I just wasn't expecting to meet you here."

"No shit you weren't expecting me. Come on."

Scheffler turned and marched away through the bunker tunnel. Frederich quickly got up and followed before Scheffler bashed the side of his fist against a button on the wall, causing a thick, metal security door to roll shut behind them.

They went through a long, pitch-black walkway which descended further and further underground before a dimly lit hallway appeared. The clicking of keys was the first thing Frederich heard. He looked left and right as they passed a long series of barely lit, bare-concrete rooms. Each one was lined with desks and computer terminals. Overlapping wires flowed in every direction, and on each leather chair sat someone either focussing on a screen, quietly talking into their headset, or furiously typing away. The walls were covered top to bottom with dozens of displays, all of them showing various surveillance footage. The scope of the place was breathtaking. Room after room after room, all dedicated to scrutinising every conceivable street, square or public area. Airport terminals appeared. Train platforms, shopping centres, even beaches were monitored. Meanwhile, nobody acknowledged Frederich. Each person remained wholly immersed in their work.

"Welcome to Intel, Abel. This is where the magic happens," said Scheffler, stretching his arms out to either side as he walked.

Frederich caught up with Scheffler and marched beside him.

"Very chic," said Frederich.

"Don't take the piss."

They passed yet another room which was the first without computer screens. It had shelves from floor to ceiling filled with all manner of weapons and equipment. Frederich paused briefly to take a closer look. There were vests, grenades, rifles, pistols, hunting knives, binoculars and various high-tech equipment, all in stacks.

"That's for later," said Scheffler without stopping.

The hallway continued as far as Frederich could see, splitting two ways in the far distance. Meanwhile, they went into a room on the right, where yet more computer screens covered the walls. Inside were eight people at their desks, their faces illuminated by the glow of their monitors. The surveillance videos on the walls were clear and crisp, revealing almost every detail. Frederich recognised The Louvre in Paris on one of the screens before it switched over to a random alleyway. Another display had a top-down view of an apartment block in what could have been Budapest or Prague.

"Team, meet Frederich Abel," said Scheffler as soon as he entered the room.

Except for one person with headphones on, the entire room stopped what they were doing and turned around. They studied Frederich curiously, looking him up and down.

Some of them seemed sceptical; others were openly smiling. One of those grinning was a freckled guy with red dreadlocks and a black bomber jacket.

"Nice," said the freckled guy with a look of wonder. "Frederich Abel, in the flesh," he added with a thick British accent.

"Let's save the ass-kissing for later," said Scheffler. "We're short on time. Abel, this is Gerricks." Scheffler signalled toward the freckled man. "Gerricks is usually with the Wealth Hunters, but we've got him leading the surveillance effort against these bastards who attacked us."

"Wealth Hunters?" said Frederich.

"Yep," cut in Gerricks. "We're the guys who make sure no one hoards too much currency. Off-shore accounts, investment properties, shares, cash, gold bars. We find it. No matter how well they hide it."

"Sounds fun," said Frederich, nodding his approval.

"As you've probably already gathered, that's not the top priority at the moment," said Scheffler. "Our surveillance teams have been flat-out gathering information about the enemy, but we're still in the early phase. We've identified dozens of them, interrogated a few. Your work in Copenhagen was a big help. We've got a ways to go before we get to Stirner, more surveillance to do, but after yesterday, we need to speed things up. They're building momentum. We have to flex."

"What do you need me to do?" said Frederich.

"We've got a special task for you," said Scheffler. "I heard you were there after the explosion at the Grand Luxus?"

Frederich frowned and nodded.

"The guy who did it. We know where he is," said Scheffler.

A current of electricity shot through Frederich's body. He lifted his head slowly and his expression hardened.

"Where?" he said.

"Gerricks. You're up," said Scheffler.

"It was a real stretch tracking that son of a bitch," said Gerricks. "He moved quickly, and changed cars before he left Germany. But like I said, nobody gets away from us. He's holed up at this apartment in Poznan, Poland." Gerricks pointed at the screen Frederich had been looking at earlier. "We don't know which apartment he's in exactly, but he hasn't left the building. That much we're sure of."

"Who is he?" asked Frederich.

Gerricks handed him a smartphone.

"All the information's on this. His name's Havel Drexler. He was Czech military before he quit and turned soldier of fortune. Did private contracts in Africa and Afghanistan for elites looking to make a profit out of chaos. Drexler specialises in hit jobs and fake terrorist attacks. He's been off the radar for a while though."

Frederich had found the images of Drexler on the smartphone and was flicking through them while listening to Gerricks. He took note of Drexler's bright-red face and scowl.

"The address where he's hiding is on there," said Gerricks. "My direct line is there too. I'll contact you if he moves while you're in transit. Whatever you need while you're in the field, you call me."

"Ok," said Frederich.

"Here's your credit card," said Gerricks. "You can use it for any necessary purchases."

Frederich took hold of a credit card with the name 'David Anders' printed on it.

"Weapons," said Gerricks. "Do you have any special requests?"

"I've got my pistol," said Frederich.

"You're a pro now, Abel," cut in Scheffler. "We've prepared a field pack for you. Stun gun, hunting knife, torch, food essentials. Anything else you need, you ask."

"Ok," said Frederich.

"Remember, this is all about sending a message," said Scheffler. "These guys need to know just how in over their heads they are. Interrogate first if you can, then go to work. Whatever you do, make it messy, and I mean *messy*. We want this felt right at the top."

Scheffler was unflinching, his dead-serious expression leaving no doubt about what he wanted.

"I'll get it done," said Frederich.

"I know you will," said Scheffler.

The room grew silent. There were no more taps on keyboards. No shuffling around. No words were spoken. All eyes were on Frederich again.

"We'll be here," said Gerricks. "Whatever you need."

"Right," said Scheffler, slamming his hand hard on Gerricks' desk, making him jump with shock. "Let's go, Abel. Thank you, gentlemen. Love your work."

Scheffler marched straight out, and Frederich followed as though Scheffler had him by a string. They went into a small room which had only a desk and one chair.

"When do I leave?" asked Frederich.

"Right away. We've got a car parked for you on the street in front of the station. Black Mini Cooper."

"Ok," said Frederich.

There was a short lull.

"Those filth," said Scheffler, suddenly spitting at the ground. "They've got no honour, do they? Killing innocent civilians like that." He looked into the distance with a scowl. "Really riles me up."

Frederich's face became hot, as he was taken back to the scene of the explosion, to the bloodied, anguished faces of the people caught up in the chaos.

"Anyway. You holding up alright?" said Scheffler. "Need anything from me before you go?"

Frederich shook his head.

"I'm fine," he said.

"Of course you are," said Scheffler.

"I did have one thing to ask," said Frederich.

"Shoot."

"How much do you know about Matthias Vidrik?"

"I know he's a traitor who doesn't have long to live. I also know you had some trouble with him."

"Yeah, he came after me."

"Why are you asking?"

"Because he didn't just go after me. He's been stalking a friend of mine here in Berlin. Ida."

"Ida? Girl?"

"Yes."

"You're worried he might go after her again? He's got other things to worry about, don't you think?"

"He's not a rational guy. I learnt that the hard way."

Scheffler sighed and nodded.

"Fair point."

"So I was wondering," said Frederich. "While I'm away, if someone can keep an eye on her?"

"She's that important?"

Frederich nodded.

34

"Yeah, she is."

"Alright. I can't have our people wasting time playing bodyguard. But if she has any problems, she can call in. I'll let Gerricks know. Tell her to use the codeword 'Abel.'"

"Ok. Thanks."

"Anything else?"

"No. That's it."

"Right. Well," said Scheffler with an encouraging nod. "Go get em'."

Frederich nodded back. He was about to turn to leave but had to ask the question.

"By the way, what's with the shirt and hair? It's not like you to be all neat and trim."

"You haven't worked it out yet? I got a bump. A big one. I'm General of Europe."

Frederich broke out smiling.

"General? Congratulations," he said.

"Don't look so happy. That means you're still under my command."

"I can handle that," said Frederich, still smiling.

"Let's see how long that lasts," said Scheffler.

On the way out they stopped by the weapons room, and Frederich picked up the backpack with his field equipment. He carefully scanned the piles of weapons one last time before snatching two tear gas grenades off the shelf and packing them into his bag. He left the bunker with the bag on his back and marched up the ramp, stomping through the shrubs then working his way out of the forest. There was no sign of the kid from earlier.

Back at Wannsee Station, he located his car and drove off, lost in thoughts about his upcoming mission. His eyes stung from fatigue and his shoulders felt stiff. His planned night of rest at home was ruined, but he barely minded. The anticipation was energising him, and it had nothing to do with excitement. He was spurred on by the prospect of slitting Havel Drexler's throat and watching him bleed to death. The thought summoned the shadow, creating a firm pressure all over Frederich's body while slowly pulling him inward into the fiery abyss. He put up no resistance, gripping the wheel harder while sensing the demon inside, itching to be unleashed. It would get its chance soon enough.

5

The passenger door opened from the outside before Francois' bald, weathered head popped in, his white goatee reaching down to his tie.

"Ready," he said.

Kalakia stepped out and adjusted his shirt. League soldiers were spread all around him, covering every entrance. The underground carpark at the Burj Khalifa was empty, except for the cars of Kalakia's two guests. In recent times, Kalakia had been escorted only by Francois and a tiny handful of rotating soldiers, typically choosing to forego having a permanent security detail. It had been unnecessary, and also would have been a sign of weakness. Kalakia's grip had been absolute, his identity and whereabouts concealed from those who had nothing to lose. Those who might have the capacity to harm him were smart enough to know better. The price paid would have been too high. As a result, The League could put its finest soldiers to better use.

Those days were now over.

With Francois leading the way, Kalakia was accompanied to the elevator by six hand-picked members of The League's Supreme Force. The door opened, and the eight of them got in. The elevator lifted seamlessly, and Kalakia observed the thick necks and broad shoulders of his men from behind, their bulletproof vests bulging through their jackets. They were handsomely paid, the security and livelihood of their families dependent on their loyalty, and most importantly, they were battle-tested. The prerequisite for entry to Supreme Force was expert-level hand-to-hand combat training, extensive military training and a minimum of ten years of field service. Their allegiance to The League and their tenacity were unquestionable.

They were also human. Kalakia could never allow Supreme Force's power to concentrate. The Ottoman Janissaries and the Roman Praetorian Guard before them had grown so overconfident that they were able to topple and replace their rulers at will. Supreme Force was a sleeping giant in much the same way. If their power superseded their duty, they would become a threat. Kalakia's solution was simple and elegant; he split Supreme Force into hundreds of splinter cells which were unaware of each other's identities. Members were occasionally moved between cells, but they never had a complete picture of the global web. Now members of Supreme Force had become Kalakia's Supreme *Guard*, and like Roman Emperors and Turkish Sultans before him, Kalakia was aware of the danger. His protectors were his potential oppressors.

The elevator reached Kalakia's penthouse, where a dozen more soldiers had secured the lobby. Kalakia could not be sure of Stirner's brazenness. Short of a daytime ground assault or fighter-jet attack on downtown Dubai, he felt he could have his meeting securely with the heads of the American and British intelligence agencies. Francois gained access to the apartment and Kalakia entered first, his Supreme 'Guard' remaining by the door.

Seated upright at the table were Charles Burley from the CIA and Georgia Tuttman of MI5. Lurking over them were League soldiers standing guard by the windows.

"Good afternoon," said Kalakia, approaching the table and taking his seat. "Excuse the delay. You will appreciate the need for added precaution. Let us skip the pleasantries and move straight to the purpose of this meeting. You know why you are here."

"Our people have already told you," said Charles Burley in his Texan accent. "The CIA has no connection or knowledge of the attacks whatsoever."

"Yes," chimed in Tuttman. "You know as well as we do that nobody in Five Eyes can afford such foolishness. And I do speak for all of our members."

Kalakia sighed while carefully studying Burscheid and Tuttman's determined faces. He then turned to Francois, who disappeared inside for a moment before emerging with two manila envelopes. Francois walked around the table and placed one in front of both people, checking to ensure he was giving the correct envelope to its intended recipient.

"What's this?" said Burley.

"Open it."

Charles Burley grasped his envelope, ripping the edge off with one clean motion. Georgia Tuttman carefully opened hers and gasped as she looked inside.

"You've got to be kidding me," said Burley.

"What is the meaning of this?" yelled Tuttman.

Burley reached into his envelope and took out the severed finger of one of his agents. He scowled in disgust and flung it onto the table, then reached into the envelope again and took out the photo of his agent sprawled on the floor with a bullet hole in his head. He looked up sharply at Kalakia.

"That's one of our men," he said. "Why did you do this?"

Tuttman now had out the photos of one of her high-ranking people, who Kalakia had ordered killed the same way.

"I want to ensure that you appreciate the seriousness of this situation. I will not tolerate complacency. You claim to have had no part in these attacks. Demonstrate your commitment to stability by helping bring these terrorists to justice."

"What terrorists?" said Tuttman, throwing up her hands. "We don't even know what you're dealing with here."

"I understand your political position," said Kalakia. "Deny all knowledge and remain neutral. Wait until the worst has passed. This would be wise under normal circumstances. However, let me assure you; these are not normal circumstances. Neutrality is not an option."

Kalakia's words ushered in a tense silence. Charles Burley began shaking his head. Georgia Tuttman sat back with her arms crossed, her face flushed red.

"This is ridiculous," muttered Burley to himself.

"Mr. Burley," said Kalakia. "If you have something on your mind, share it. But I warn you, be careful with your words. My tolerance is running dangerously low after the events in Berlin."

Kalakia and his fellow titan faced off. Burley's hands were quivering, his nostrils flared. Kalakia dug into him with his stare, sensing himself nearing the edge. He and Burley both possessed enough firepower to devastate the other completely, except it was the Americans with the most to lose. The United States could cripple The League any time they chose, but the cost to them would be so colossal that they would never attempt it. The ensuing conflict would shatter the world economy and destabilise society for years. The modern world was a machine whose momentum was not permitted to stop, and it was Kalakia who had his finger on the off-switch. He was not looking to go to war with the global powers. That would be suicide. It was Stirner he wanted. Yet since the attack on the Grand Luxus, his darker impulses had risen like evil spirits, and he found himself close to the point of no return. His desire to lash out was almost irresistible. From the moment the explosion went off in Berlin, Kalakia knew he would annihilate anyone who did not cooperate.

Georgia Tuttman uncrossed her arms and leaned forward.

"Tell us what you need, and I'll see what MI5 can do," she said.

Kalakia extended his fingers out to release the tension and took a deep, calming breath. He nodded at Francois to hand Tuttman the next envelope. Tuttman opened it and began sifting through the photos of Stirner as Burley reluctantly reached out and snatched his envelope from Francois' hand.

"Both of you know who Horst Stirner is," said Kalakia. "It is in everyone's best interest to locate him quickly. If we do not, then this conflict will escalate, and innocent people will die. There will be more disruption caused to the global economy than at any time since the Second World War. This act of terrorism in Berlin is only the beginning."

"Ok," said Tuttman. "We'll keep an eye out for him. Anything else?"

Kalakia recalled Stirner's words. *You forgot to look in the shadows.*

"Yes," he said. "I want profiles on your most wanted criminals, and I want them by midnight tonight. I expect your partners in the Five Eyes to cooperate, as well as all nations you collaborate with."

"Which criminals exactly?" said Burley. "This is a long list you're talking about."

"Use your common sense. I have no interest in wife killers and petty thieves. Focus on those who are capable of extreme violence. Those associated with organised crime and drug cartels, anyone on your terror watch list, those associated with guerrilla groups, and so forth."

"You think this is blowback from the underworld?" asked Tuttman, leaning forward while rubbing her chin.

"Yes. The League has extinguished their influence over the years. Our demise opens the door for them to reassert control."

"I can give you a list of influential figures who would have plenty of motivation to want you dead," said Tuttman.

"While we have given the world's elites ample reason to support Stirner, they are not the tip of the spear. We must address the threat directly."

"There's no way we can meet your deadline," interjected Burley.

Kalakia leaned back and steepled his fingers.

"Is that so?" he said. "Your collective is the single most efficient espionage alliance ever devised, with almost a century of cooperation. You are above national law, able to act with total impunity. You have coordinated countless coups, brought down numerous governments, and you have outclassed the Soviet Union. I trust you can scrape together some documents in one day."

"Why are you coming to us?" said Tuttman. "The League's intelligence is second to none. You've already taken our brightest people, and your technology is light-years ahead of ours."

"Ms. Tuttman, The League has co-existed with your respective governments for almost three decades because we know our mission. We police inequality, and we do so because you cannot, or rather, will not. We are the only line of defence against greed and corruption. Policing your criminals was never our job. As a result, many have slipped through our net. This was a critical mistake, but be assured we will correct it. In the meantime, global stability is at stake. The files, by midnight. Otherwise I will count you as an enemy and will act accordingly. None of your people will be safe."

"Fine," said Tuttman.

Burley bit on his lower lip and looked down at the table.

"Mr. Burley," said Kalakia with a firm voice.

"We'll get you what you need," said Burley.

"Good. Then that will be all. Unless you have further questions?"

Nobody spoke.

"Time is ticking. Francois will show you out."

Francois signalled the way to the door with an open palm, and after a short hesitation, the pair stood and allowed him to usher them out.

A short time later Francois was at Kalakia's side, while Kalakia remained occupied with the view of the Dubai skyline, which was sweltering under the afternoon sun. Francois remained patiently waiting with his hands clasped behind his back.

"It's time," said Kalakia after some time. "Convene a council of war."

"When?"

"In two days. At the fortress."

Francois prepared to walk away.

"Wait," said Kalakia, still looking out of the window. "What of the bomber?"

"He's still hiding in Poland. Scheffler gave the job to Frederich."

Kalakia hesitated for a moment, gripped by a sudden tension in his chest. Then he nodded, and Francois' footsteps disappeared out of the room. Kalakia considered this latest development. He understood Scheffler's reasoning. The question was: would Frederich be able to cope with the wartime pressure? Perhaps it would be best to test him further in the field with a low-stakes assignment. Then Kalakia thought better of it. For what he had in mind, Frederich was exactly what was needed. In the worst case, Frederich would snap and unleash hell. Kalakia had no objections to that, not after what Stirner had done in Berlin. An unhinged Frederich fit perfectly into Kalakia's plan. It would remind Stirner and anyone who supported him of the consequences of threatening The League.

For a time Kalakia descended further into the dark, twisted areas of his mind, imagining the brutal ways he could humiliate and punish Stirner. Finally, he went into his study with the sudden urge to refresh his reading on Otto von Bismarck.

6

Not again, thought Ida, her face and body growing hot and sticky. She was back in the vacuum with the screaming voices. Her eyes darted all around, desperate for a way to escape. There was too much to absorb. The wails from the people kept coming, begging for an end to the agony. She could hear them inside her head. There was nowhere to hide, nothing to shield her. She remembered how holding Frederich's hand had helped her, steadied her, kept her from being devoured by terror.

A warm hand touched her neck and drew her out of her torment. She welcomed it, and focussed on how it felt; gentle, firm, reassuring. The vacuum began dissolving, giving way to the murmurs of the flea market crowd. The sunshine on her arm was next to break into her consciousness. Meanwhile, her breathing grew fuller and penetrated deeper.

"You alright?" said Chi, removing her hand from Ida's neck and rubbing her shoulder.

Ida blinked multiple times and forced a smile.

"Yes, I.."

"You were thinking about the explosion?"

Ida nodded.

"It's ok. Look," said Chi, opening the metallic money box stuffed with notes. "We're getting paid. The Virgin Queen Collection is taking off."

Ida looked blankly at the container, wondering how money would make it 'ok.'

"Stay with me today," said Chi. "Our lovely customers need you."

"Of course," said Ida, now slightly more convinced. "We can't let the customers down."

"That's right."

Ida reached over the table and began tidying up the pieces of clothing that had been shuffled around by curious hands. It was the middle of the afternoon, and the people at the Bergmannstrasse Flea Market in Kreuzberg were shoulder to shoulder. The odd person sauntered by, giving the clothes a sceptical stare before moving along. The stall to Ida's left was offering a mishmash of household antiques, including spoons, knives and decorative plates. There was also a collection of 19th-century-style wooden globes, which made Ida think back on her journey across the world to Berlin. The sun, the crowd, the turmoil inside her, it was still hard to believe how far she had come in a year, let alone what she had overcome.

"Ida, look!"

Chi was pointing toward a particular young girl in the crowd with long flowing black hair. She was wearing the cream overalls which Ida had designed. Ida gasped in delight.

"Oh, wow," she whispered to herself.

The girl noticed Ida and Chi looking at her and she waved, pointing proudly toward her overalls and tensing her bicep before proceeding to do a brief jig. Chi and Ida burst out laughing and waved back, and the girl rejoined her friends and disappeared into the crowd.

"I knew those would be popular," said Chi.

Ida remained smiling until her cheeks grew sore. Suddenly she remembered the people at the scene of the explosion, and an intense wave of guilt washed over her. The smile disappeared, and she grew serious again.

"Chrissi just messaged," said Chi, looking at her smartphone. "She said they'll be here a bit later, just as soon as Daria wakes up. Who knows what time they got home last night."

"Probably late," said Ida. "They never leave a party before 8:00 am."

The song lyrics suddenly played back in her head in German: '*You're crazy my child, you must go to Berlin.*'

"We need to pack soon, maybe tell them to meet us at your place instead?" said Ida, thinking ahead.

"We'll work it out when Sleeping Beauty wakes up," said Chi, looking up from her phone as a shadow appeared over the table.

An olive-skinned woman in her thirties had approached and was browsing through the freshly folded pieces of clothing. She had an intimidating face, along with exceptional posture and straight, shiny-black, shoulder-length hair. With her gaze narrowed and her red lipstick-covered lips pressed together, she searched sceptically through the pieces on the table. Her outfit was immaculate; including a white silk shirt, black satin blazer and pants, and black stilettos. She was not from Berlin, Ida decided. Probably on a business trip and curious about the 'alternative' side of the city. The woman held up one of Ida's earliest designs for inspection; the white shirt inspired by Elizabeth I.

"These are.. interesting," said the woman, hesitating for a moment. "Not boring, to say the least."

"Boring isn't inspiring," said Ida.

The woman shot Ida a sharp glance, then looked again at the shirt, staring earnestly at the broad frilly arms and decorated collar.

"Can I try it on?"

"We don't have anywhere to change here, but you can bring it back if it doesn't fit. We come every week."

"Yes, friends of mine have bought your clothes," said the woman. "They were talking about you yesterday over dinner. One of them suggested I drop by and take a look."

"I hope they were happy with everything," said Ida.

"I wouldn't be here otherwise, would I?" said the woman.

"You're a small, right?" Chi chimed in.

"Usually, yes," said the woman. "You never know with these brands. They fake sizes all the time, trying to fool you into thinking you're skinner than you are. "

"Show me," said Chi, taking the shirt and holding it up in front of her. "Yep, that'll fit. But as Ida said, you can bring it back if you're not happy."

"Ok, fine. I'll take it."

The woman made her purchase, putting the shirt into her handbag.

"Thank you, ladies," she said. "And thank you, Ida," she added, looking deeply into Ida's eyes.

Ida blushed and smiled back before the woman turned and marched away, the heels of her stilettos clacking loudly over the concrete.

The woman's intoxicating presence lingered for a while, and Ida could not help but be reminded of María Félix, penetrating the environment with her sexuality and beauty. A person later approached and browsed for a long time before they smiled politely and left. Ida then turned and noticed Chi frowning and looking into the distance.

"What is it?" said Ida.

"Creep alert," said Chi.

The words sucked the wind out of Ida. *Vidrik.* She backed away and took shelter behind Chi, not daring to look. Somehow she managed to turn her eyes in the direction Chi was staring. When she saw him, she grew giddy with relief. Frederich was standing against the wall of the pharmacy with one leg crossed over the other while looking directly at Ida and Chi.

"I'll be back in a minute," said Ida.

"What, you know that guy?"

"Yes. I'll explain later."

Ida handed the money box over to Chi and walked out from behind the stall and weaved her way through the crowd.

"Hi," said Frederich with a shy grin when she approached.

"Hey," said Ida, stepping forward and giving him a hug.

"Sorry for just showing up like this. You told me you were here on Sundays."

"No," said Ida, shaking her head. "It's fine. We didn't get a chance to talk after…"

"Yeah," said Frederich as Ida trailed off. "How are you?"

"I don't know," said Ida with a shrug. "I'm still dealing with it, I think. How about you?"

"I'm fine," said Frederich calmly, looking briefly into the distance.

"That's good."

"I just came to see you because I have to go away for a few days, maybe more."

"Ok," said Ida, trying to conceal her suspicious thoughts. *Where are you going, Frederich?*

"We also didn't get a chance to finish the Vidrik conversation."

"Was there anything more to say?" said Ida.

Frederich reached into his pocket and took out a folded piece of paper.

"As far as we know, Vidrik's not in the country, and he'll have to think twice before coming back to Berlin." Frederich held out the piece of paper. "But just in case, here's a number you can call if anything happens while I'm gone. If you feel someone following you, or anything out of the ordinary, you can call in."

Ida took the piece of paper and opened it.

"Codeword: Abel? Whose number is this?"

"It's League Intel. They can send someone if you ask."

Ida studied the piece of paper for a long time.

"I don't know about this," she said, holding the paper at a distance and leaning back as though it were infected with something.

"Ida, take it. Kalakia promised you'd be safe, so this has to be his way to keep that promise."

Ida sighed and lowered her hand.

"If it were up to me, you would go back home until we found him," said Frederich.

"I'm not going to do that."

"I know."

Ida sighed again, then nodded.

"Ok. I'll call if I need it."

"Thanks," said Frederich. "That makes me feel better."

"Should I ask where you're going?" said Ida.

Frederich gave a slight squint, appearing hesitant.

"It depends. You wanted me to be honest with you. But you also don't want anything to do with my work."

"That's right. Does it have something to do with the bombing?"

"Yes," said Frederich.

Ida shuddered.

"You know who did it," she said flatly.

"Yes."

Ida now sensed herself treading into darker territory. Reading Frederich's voice and expression, she knew he would be going to kill the person responsible. How did she feel about that? Did she want that person dead? Yes, she did. Of course, she did. They deserved to die. *No!* How could she think that? Her cheeks burnt up, and she felt unsteady on her feet.

"I don't want to know anymore," she said, holding her palm up.

"Sure," said Frederich. "It's going to be fine, ok?"

"I need to get back to the stall."

"Ok. See you when I get back?" asked Frederich, leaning his head expectantly.

"I.. I need to get back. Bye, Frederich."

She turned around, nearly bumping into a man behind her who stopped walking abruptly and gave her an annoyed stare. She went around him and marched back toward Chi.

"Ok, I have questions," said Chi. "Because that guy is cute. Creepy, but cute."

Once Ida was back on the other side of the table, the hot flush in her face subsided as though she were out of the danger zone. She looked across toward the pharmacy, but Frederich was already gone.

"Ida, spill it. Who is he?"

"What?" said Ida, still distracted.

"I said who's the guy?"

"He's a friend."

"And?"

"And we need to start packing."

"Ugh! You're impossible," said Chi, slapping Ida's shoulder softly. "Sometimes I think *you're* the Virgin Queen."

Chi walked around Ida and began taking the clothes off the table and placing them in their boxes. Ida went over next to her and started helping, trying to push the idea of Frederich committing murder out of her mind. Her body felt cold now, as she recalled the look in Frederich's eyes while she questioned him. He was so calm that it spooked her. She hated that side of him, loathed being around it. It got under her skin, seeped inside her like thick black smoke which blurred her thoughts. As long as Vidrik was lurking out there, she had no choice but to tolerate it. After the danger passed, she would have to seriously rethink having Frederich in her life. *See you when I get back,* he had said. As though they were friends or something! Like he was going on a short trip to visit family. Damn him and his stupid, violent friends, she thought. Vidrik too, and his sick, twisted mind. Innocent people had died because of The League Of Reckoning, and now Frederich thought he could solve everything by adding to the death toll.

Ida was barely breathing now, and was stuffing the clothes into the boxes with too much force. She slammed the box shut, fighting with the flaps, then picked it up and thrust it onto the pile with a thump, causing Chi to give her a long, questioning stare. Ida giggled suddenly. It felt good to be angry, to let off some steam. If Vidrik showed up, she would let him have some of it.

Maybe violence *was* the answer, she thought. Well, sometimes, anyway. It had to have been put there for a reason in any case.

7

Somewhere behind that arched, stained antique door was Havel Drexler; the terrorist behind the Berlin Bombing.

Frederich stood in the middle of the quaint, cobbled street in the old town of Poznan while a stream of pedestrians casually worked their way around him. He was expecting a bright idea to come, a way to flush Drexler out or to get him into a position to make the kill. It was a chilly, overcast day, and Frederich zipped up his thick, black parka jacket. Tucked inside were his pistol and hunting knife, as well as two tear gas grenades. He lingered for a while, then figured there were better places to wait for inspiration to hit. Standing there was inviting Drexler to spot him out. The solution would come to him soon enough. It always did.

He went over to a cafe forty feet away across the street. While waiting for his espresso, he checked his smartphone for updates from Intel. There was nothing. Instead, he started flicking through Drexler's photos. The headshot showed a man with unsympathetic eyes, flushed skin and puffy cheeks. Another snap had a younger, fitter Drexler in military uniform standing in a dusty, African town with a Heckler & Koch held across his torso and the same grim stare. Whichever way Frederich decided to proceed, he could expect to meet someone with ample experience in weaponry and explosives, as well as the readiness to use them at any moment day or night.

The espresso came, and Frederich took a sip while turning his attention to the apartment block. It was a two-storey building, so he was not surprised at the lack of movement coming in or out. He settled in for the afternoon, eventually ordering another espresso, and remained watching the street. Nothing out of the ordinary occurred, except when a blonde woman left the building and came back with two young boys below the age of ten. She tussled with her keys as the boys chased each other in circles before they all went inside. Maybe it was the caffeine, or perhaps the pent up agitation from the bombing, but eventually Frederich felt the urge to act. Kraas' voice of reason popped into his head: *It's too risky to go inside. Wait. The opening will come.* Frederich dismissed the idea. Enough was enough. It was time to take a closer look.

'David Anders' paid with his credit card then left the cafe. He stood some distance from the front door and tried to look uninterested, stealing the occasional glance of the building. 3:45 pm. The workday was finishing, meaning somebody would have to come in or out. The door remained shut for some time further. Finally, a tall, dark-haired woman with a light grey trench coat and high heels shoes slowed down in front of the door while searching inside her hand-bag. Frederich braced himself, taking a step in her direction, before the woman took out her lighter and lit a cigarette. Frederich relaxed again, somewhat disappointed, then the door suddenly swung open from the inside, giving him a jolt. He scrambled forward and caught the door at the same time a man with dark cornrows and tattoo-covered neck stormed out. The man slowed down when he noticed

Frederich, and the two of them locked eyes. The chances of the man being with Drexler were high, but Frederich had to be careful not to give himself away. He smiled at the man with a nod and continued inside. He immediately reached into the seam of his jacket and grasped his pistol as the door slammed shut behind him. He took the safety off. Each second felt like five, and his ears remained trained at the door. The occasional playful yell or laugh came from outside along with the sound of people shuffling by. The door remained shut, and as more time passed, the sense of danger gradually died away. Frederich flicked the safety back on. His breathing returned to normal. He knew he would look harmless enough to the man. With such a small building he would have at least roused the man's suspicion, so better to be cautious than dead. He turned his attention back to the task of finding Drexler.

The lobby was brightly lit from the back by a stained window decorated with detailed floral patterns of yellow, red, purple and green. More floral shapes intricately adorned the curved, bronze staircase leading to the second floor. The building had inherited an almost sacred quality from an earlier century, seemingly shrouded with divine light which Frederich's shadow soon contaminated as he crept forward.

There were two apartments across from each other on the bottom floor. Frederich approached the left one first. It was dead quiet inside. *Maybe.* He went over to the opposite apartment, which had a shoe rack at the front with only women's shoes on it. Drexler could have been hiding out with a girlfriend, he thought. He moved away from the door and climbed the elaborate, curved staircase to the top floor, where there were two more apartments. The smell of cooking hung in the air. The sounds of children screaming excitedly at each other came from the right, and the left apartment had its front door open. A vacuum cleaner turned on, causing loud whirring to invade the hallway, while the head of the vacuum cleaner protruded outside to clean the welcome mat. Frederich turned around and went back downstairs. He stood undecided in the light in the middle of the lobby. The silence of the first apartment made it strangely alluring, and Frederich found himself slowly creeping toward it, taking gentle, careful steps while listening for any intervening clues inside.

Scratching noises came from the front of the building. Frederich turned his head quickly, seeing a shadow beneath the crack of the door, and he rushed to a position behind the stairs. The outside door flung open, bringing the street noise in with it. It remained suspended, held open by the foot of the tattooed man from earlier. The man took the keys out of the hole and picked up two duffel bags, the strain of their weight showing on his arms. He then skewed left and dropped the bags onto the floor in front of the silent apartment. Upon unlocking and pushing the door open, he picked up his bags and disappeared inside before the apartment door slammed shut, and Frederich was left alone again inside a lifeless lobby.

He remained thinking in his spot. He was now almost sure that Drexler was in that apartment. Whatever the man was carrying in those bags, it was not business documents or groceries. The guy had some serious hardware in there. Despite that, Frederich wanted to be positive. He opened the back door and went into the yard; a tiny, fenced-off area with an entrance to the underground cellar beside a set of garbage and recycling bins. Each of the apartments had windows looking out into the yard, and Frederich checked them carefully before crawling in beside the bins and training his eyes on the first apartment. It had four windows; one from the kitchen, a small bathroom window, and the rest likely the living and bedrooms. Frederich waited and watched as the first hour ticked by, then the second, before eventually darkness set in and the lights inside the apartment went on. All the curtains were drawn, but Frederich could see the occasional shadow moving between the gaps. At one point the back door to the building broke open, and a heavy-set older woman came out holding a full garbage bag. Frederich shrunk deeper into the corner, and the woman thrust the bag into the bin and slammed the lid shut before walking back, mumbling something to herself in Polish.

Frederich sat patiently in the dark like a fox, alert but barely moving, sensing himself merging into the night as the time passed by and his anticipation slowly grew. From his position in the corner, he got the break he was looking for. If he had lost his focus for even a few seconds, he might have missed it. Without warning, one of the curtains was dragged open and someone appeared with a lit cigarette in his mouth. Frederich skipped a breath. That red, round face stood out like a match head. Drexler rolled the window open slightly with the crank handle, and as soon as he had appeared he was gone. Midnight approached, and the lights went out.

Frederich lingered in the shadows until 3:30 am with unbridled, festering thoughts, unable to stop his mind going back to the day of the bombing. The screams, the carnage; Ida and the innocent civilians, overwhelmed with suffering. Frederich's rage resonated in his fingers, his legs grew restless. The pressure in his chest sucked the air out of him. That son of a bitch — the cause of it all — was inside that apartment, sleeping soundly. What was Frederich waiting for? 'Make it messy,' Scheffler had said. *My pleasure,* thought Frederich.

He rose out of the corner and marched out. First, he pushed the lobby door open and lodged it on the clip. Now the front door of Drexler's apartment would remain in view. Frederich walked back into the yard and took out his pistol and a tear gas grenade. He fired a bullet at the living room window, the loud snap of the suppressor shattering the peaceful, morning silence. Shards of glass came crashing to the ground as he walked across and fired another bullet into the bedroom window. Using his pistol hand, he removed the pin from the tear gas grenade, shifted the curtain to the side and tossed in the grenade. Then he walked back across and followed it up by tossing another grenade into the living room. The tear gas rose up and gradually began filling the apartment. He took ten steps backwards and pointed his pistol into the white cloud while keeping the front door to the apartment in his sights.

Two distinct yells came from inside as smoke poured out of the window. Frederich focussed ahead, ready to snatch the life out of anybody moving inside. A shadow appeared, then disappeared, then flashed again at the left side before the front door burst open. It was the tattooed man with the cornrows who Frederich had seen earlier. The man bent over in the middle of the lobby, wearing tracksuit pants and a white singlet, coughing and rubbing his eyes. Frederich marched toward him and fired a bullet into his skull on approach, then followed it up with another headshot at point-blank range, showering the lobby floor with blood. Drexler was the next to come bursting out. Frederich heard his groan before he emerged wearing only boxer shorts. His shoulder ricocheted off the doorway, and he went tumbling. As he lay helpless on the floor, Frederich sent a stiff, forceful kick into his side.

"Ah!" yelled Drexler, filling the lobby with his screams.

He rolled over and clutched his side with one arm, groaning and rubbing his irritated eyes with the other. Frederich glanced at the neighbour's apartment. The door remained closed, the person inside having the good sense not to come outside. It also meant they would be cowered somewhere near a telephone, terrified and desperate for the police to arrive. Frederich had to move quickly. He dropped his pistol the ground.

"Drexler!" he yelled, bending down and grasping Drexler's sweaty face by his cheeks.

"No!" yelled Drexler, struggling to break free of Frederich's grip. His eyes were teared up, and his nostrils full of mucus.

Frederich picked up his pistol again, aimed it at Drexler's knee cap, and fired.

The metallic echoes of the bullet fire were horrifyingly loud, piecing Frederich's eardrums. Drexler's screaming became hysterical. Frederich put the pistol down again.

"Look here!" he yelled, grasping Drexler's face again with an iron grip. "Eyes here, you piece of shit."

He held Drexler's head in place and stared into his swollen eyes. Drexler's yells became a wail, and he was eventually able to lock onto Frederich's face for a moment. Once Frederich was sure that Drexler could see him, he looked deep into Drexler's eyes and poured in all the hatred he could conjure. Drexler paused, his eyes opening wide against the tear gas spasms trying to force them shut. The message seemed to have come across.

"I'm sorry!" he screamed at the top of his lungs, beginning to hyperventilate. "I had no choice. It hurt too much. It was too much!"

Drexler began weeping and howling. Frederich let go of his head and backed away, leaving the pistol on the ground. He looked on, speechless, unsure what to do next. Drexler seemed to be hallucinating, grasping at the air and talking to himself.

The flicker of the shooter's shadow probably saved Frederich's life. He had likely been holed up in the bathroom, waiting for the smoke to disperse. Frederich turned quickly and leapt to the side just as the man fired from the doorway. Frederich's pistol was out of reach. Instead, he ran away at a sharp angle as the second bullet flew by, then went straight at the shooter and jump-kicked him. The two of them went tumbling to the floor, the man grunting as he collided with the surface. The shooter was still holding his pistol, and he lifted his hand to fire. Frederich took hold of his wrist, and with the memory of Elias Khartoum flickering by, he head-butted him in the nose once and then twice. The man let go of the pistol.

It came, hurtling from the beyond, and Frederich knew it was too late to catch it. Not that he ever had a chance. It came on so strongly that the blackouts began almost immediately. He knew he had done damage with his fists, and that he had used the hunting knife. The rest came in visual and audible flashes. Drexler's horrible screams. The sound of flesh tearing. The pools of blood, as well as the dark red imprints from Frederich's footsteps as he fled the building. There was the piercing ringing in his ears as he stumbled down the street and marched quickly to his car. He blacked out again in places, and when he came to, he was sitting in the driver's seat soaked in blood. He took out his keys and worked them into the hole with strangely steady hands. He put the car into gear and drove away, racing to the end of the small street and making a hard left. Police sirens in the distance forced him to speed up. He did everything by instinct, following the directions he had studied, eventually climbing onto the 92 and racing westwards toward Berlin.

8

The faces of Kalakia's Four Generals glowed orange in the candlelight, while a thick layer of cigar smoke hung above the empty weapons storage room. A chilly, early-morning breeze pushed through the cave tunnel of The League's mountain fortress, causing the candles along the walls to flicker. Kalakia was leaned over with his hands flat on the table, inspecting the world map spread over its surface. Red crosses marked the spots where Stirner had carried out his initial attacks. Berlin was also marked. In green were the places where The League proposed to counter-attack. Each of the Four Generals possessed a portion of the list of targets provided by the Five Eyes. In the back corner, Francois was slumped on a chair with one leg crossed over the other, supporting his neck from behind with his hand.

"Gentlemen, we have decisions to make," said Kalakia.

Marco Lessio leaned back casually on his chair and sucked on his cigar before contributing to the cloud of smoke hovering above them. The shadow of Daps Limbaba's intimidating frame stretched over the table, where he had his elbow resting with his cigar pointing outwards, a heap of ashes piled up beneath it. He stared unflinchingly at Kalakia with absolute focus. Tamju Lau rubbed on his greying moustache and cleared his throat.

"I agree that we must act," said Lau. "I only fear that Stirner has a greater plan which we have yet to comprehend."

"He's shitting his pants," said Lessio. "He messed up the Kalakia hit, so he's lost the element of surprise. Now he's relying on terror tactics. We need to hit hard and finish him quickly."

"My men await my word. They are ready for anything," said Limbaba.

Kalakia paused then turned to the quietest General in the room.

"Vincent?" he said.

Scheffler had been sitting forward, tapping his fingers on the table while deep in thought.

"I've got concerns," he said. "Suspicion's growing. The online chatter is way too loud. Plus tributes aren't being paid. Word's going around that The League is losing authority. We've worked too hard to let this bastard take it away from us. Our pride's at stake here."

"You have a right to be concerned," said Kalakia. "Our spies tell us the elite are publicly speaking out against us. Recent events have emboldened them."

"I've already told my soldiers to make an example of anyone who doesn't pay," said Marco Lessio.

"This will not solve the deeper problem," said Daps Limbaba. "We must cure the disease, not attend to the symptoms."

"I think Kalakia's idea makes sense," said Scheffler. "Our surveillance on government and public figures is airtight, which means Stirner's using the underworld for muscle. We take the list and we strike hard, all at once. We'll make those bastards sing. When the dust settles, we'll know what we're dealing with, and we can round up the string pullers. Stirner won't have anywhere to hide after that."

"You do not appear convinced, Tamju," said Kalakia, turning toward Lau, who was rubbing his chin and frowning.

"I have an unsettling feeling," said Lau. "There are sinister forces at play."

"What do you suggest?" said Kalakia.

"Caution," said Lau, his eyes lighting up. "Utmost caution."

The ominous nature of Lau's shift in mood gripped the entire table. Marco Lessio sat forward and studied the proud-statured old man.

"We find ourselves in unprecedented territory," said Kalakia after a long silence. "Our enemy knows us far better than we know him."

"You know Stirner. What's your guess about what he's up to?" said Scheffler.

Kalakia looked away, focussing on one of the candles flickering in the distance. The League was as powerful as a firestorm where it counted but could be as fragile as a tiny flame in the fickle minds of the masses. One wrong move and the tide of public opinion would turn, sending through a gust of wind that would put out The League's light. Kalakia was the man holding The League together. The flame continued to burn because he was on the throne, and he succeeded by remaining a step ahead. The League's survival hinged on his capacity to outmanoeuvre Stirner.

Meanwhile, the longer he waited, the more fragile The League's flame would become. With Inselheim in Stirner's hands, it was only a matter of time before the geopolitical balance tipped in Stirner's favour and the gust found its way to Kalakia. Morale and momentum were everything. As leader, his role was to remain steadfast in the face of uncertainty. The fate of The League depended on it. He turned back to his Generals.

"Stirner is a cunning man, driven by power and prestige," he said. "His ego is fickle and infested with hubris. That will be his downfall. He plans to slay The League and establish his own global empire over its ashes."

"Not going to happen," said Marco Lessio, scowling and making a tight fist.

"He will be the first and the last to challenge us," said Limbaba.

"We have a slim window to avoid catastrophe," said Kalakia. "And we must make the most of it. Show of hands who supports the counter-attack."

All four men raised their hands. Kalakia completed the vote by raising his.

He turned his attention to the map again. New York, Zurich, Doha, Tokyo, Cape Town. Stirner had gone global with his surprise attack. He had wanted to demoralise The League by cutting off its head while inflicting significant damage. The attacks were evenly spread, and information about the origins of the attackers was scarce at best. Stirner had used his intimate knowledge of The League with deadly effect while conspiring with Navolov and likely other members of the leadership. The attackers had struck with ski masks and mostly retreated without a trace. Kalakia's hunch that there had been only a few traitors proved correct — otherwise, a revolt would have broken out when he annihilated The Generals and The Council, and he would be a dead man. As always, Kalakia bet that power was with the people. He was proven correct. The foundation on which he had built The League remained solid.

"Our objective is to uncover the scope of our enemy," said Kalakia. "Strike quickly, and move your targets to a secure interrogation facility. Kill only when necessary."

"What if we get a lead? Do we follow it or wait?" asked Marco Lessio.

The question highlighted a serious dilemma. The surprise nature of the first wave was aimed at reducing casualties, after which Stirner's people would be on red alert.

"Report it to Intel, then pursue," said Kalakia.

The table seemed satisfied.

"I believe Francois has some good news for us from Poland," said Kalakia, turning to the corner.

Francois sat up and cleared his throat.

"The Berlin bomber is dead," he said coldly. "Frederich Abel terminated him this morning."

"Wonderful!" said Daps Limbaba while slapping the table with his mighty hand.

"Spit out the details," said Scheffler. "Everybody needs to know."

Francois wrinkled his brows and his face turned grim.

"Abel terminated Drexler and two of his associates with utmost prejudice. The news reported over thirty stab wounds on one of the victims. The city is in total shock."

Kalakia studied the reactions of his Generals. Marco Lessio was licking his lower lip and smiling. Daps Limbaba narrowed his eyes and was nodding repeatedly. Tamju Lau stared off into the distance.

"If that doesn't send a lightning bolt up Stirner's ass, I don't know what will," said Scheffler.

"Why have you done this?" Tamju Lau asked Scheffler. "Where is the honour in such madness?"

"Honour?" said Scheffler. "Do you want to discuss honour with the families of Drexler's victims? How about all those mutilated people laying in hospital beds? Or how about the fact that they killed our brothers and tried to assassinate our leader?"

"Senseless barbarity only begets more barbarity," said Lau calmly. "A bullet to the head would have sufficed."

"Where did you get this kid, anyway?" Marco Lessio asked Kalakia. "We haven't met, but I like him already."

Kalakia sighed and leaned back in his chair.

"The boy is an anomaly. He is skilled beyond imagination, yet he is gripped by dark forces."

"Whatever," said Lessio with a shrug. "He's exactly what we need right now."

"I agree," said Kalakia. "War is not kind to those who do not reciprocate the brutality of their enemy."

"Abel's warrior spirit will carry us to victory," said Limbaba with fire in his eyes. "There is no stopping us."

Kalakia felt satisfied with his Generals' response to the news of Drexler's brutal demise. His hope that the boy's unorthodox methods would excite the men had come true. Frederich's heinous deeds were acting as a call to arms for the soldiers.

"Strike time is two days from now," said Kalakia. "Thursday, 3:00 am, Central European Time. Any objections?"

Only the flicker of candles could be heard. Francois cleared his throat in the corner and shuffled around.

"Discretion is everything," said Kalakia, raising his voice to emphasise the importance of his message. "We strike as one. No rogue acts — do nothing which might prematurely compromise the plan. Any leaks could prove devastating. Put your soldiers on alert, but do not share specific details with them until the day of the attacks." One by one, Kalakia stared sharply at each of his Generals. "Is that understood?" he said.

Each man nodded obediently.

"Prepare for battle, gentlemen."

Frederich jerked the steering wheel abruptly and pulled over to the side of the road, left the door open behind him and dashed into the overgrown grass. He began retching immediately, each contraction sending a sharp ache through his ribs and waist. Because he had barely eaten, his purge produced only dark bile.

The nausea eased somewhat, but he still felt weak in the legs. He collapsed onto his knees, moaning and bending his head to the ground. It took all of his strength to keep his eyes open, to avoid going back into flashback mode, but the pull of the abyss was too much. He fell backwards onto the grass, closed his eyes and went into the black. There he was met by Drexler, squirming and screaming hysterically. Images of bloodied, mutilated flesh flickered by, then a thick, dark red pool oozed across the floor. The groans of the shooter by the door sounded unnatural, like an animal in distress. Frederich quickly opened his eyes. It was too much to take in at once. He looked down with disgust at his shirt, which was soiled in the blood of his slaughtered foes. At first he pulled at it, then stretched it out, desperately trying to get it off. The stitching gave out at the side before he managed to pull the shirt off, only to find that his skin was also stained red.

The surrounding area was secluded, with no sign of people and no houses. In the distance was a brown wooden fence which separated the vast plot of country land, and beyond that was a small lake. Frederich stomped shirtless through the grass in the direction of the water. He reached the fence and grasped it, bending his body over and flipping to the other side, crashing down onto his shoulder. The impact re-aggravated the bruising from Vidrik's sniper bullet and sucked the air out of him. After hesitating briefly, he rolled to his side and forced himself up, then limped onwards to the lake and trudged straight into the water.

He dove under. The shock of the cold passed quickly, and he remained submerged for a long time with his eyes closed. The effect was instant. His state of weightlessness relieved him of the pain, the upward force of the water holding him in place without reservation or judgement. He went deeper into the feeling as his oxygen slowly ran out. The pressure in his lungs grew while he advanced further into the abyss. For a moment he lost touch with his body and experienced absolute calm. He remained hovering in the silence before his feet pushed into the mud and he emerged out of the water while sucking in an enormous gulp of air. Once he caught his breath again, he floated on his back and gazed up at the grey sky, rejuvenated and soaked in relief.

9

Footsteps approached Inselheim's room from outside and stopped in front of the door. There was clattering in the key-hole before the door swung open, revealing one of the guards, dressed in neat army green trousers and a button-up shirt, just like all the others Inselheim had seen. Beside the guard was an older man with silver hair and a round belly, wearing tan chinos and a navy blue polo shirt. The guard remained by the door, and the man walked inside by himself, taking slow, purposeful steps. Inselheim had been resting on his king-sized bed, where his kidnappers had imprisoned him in a luxurious room for the past two days, and he sat up at attention. The man gave Inselheim a dry smile, his eyes barely moving.

"Hello, Mr. Inselheim," said the man. "My name is Horst Stirner."

Inselheim gave the man careful attention but said nothing. It was yet another unexpected development in a baffling series of days.

"Have you been well looked after?" said Stirner after the long pause. "I told my guards to treat you with the respect that a man of your stature deserves. Please tell me if they fail in their duty."

Respect? thought Inselheim. They had tossed him into the back of a moving van, blindfolded him and tightly bound his hands and feet. Then they left him there for almost a day wondering when he would die or how badly they would torture him when they stopped.

"You're kidding," said Inselheim. His neck still ached from being jammed up against the side of the van. His wrists were bruised and scabbed from where the cable tie had cut into them. "Do you know what I've been through?"

"It is unfortunate what happened to you," said Stirner. "To save you from The League Of Reckoning, we needed to act quickly and decisively. We couldn't worry about your well-being until we had you safe and secure. If we're honest, it was The League who did most of the damage. It was not us who extorted and tortured you, remember."

Inselheim opened his mouth to speak again, then stopped. He considered what this man Stirner had said.

"How do you know about all that?" he asked. "About The League."

"Because I am a former member of its Council."

"You're not with them?"

"Not anymore."

"Why not?"

"Because I could no longer bear the hypocrisy."

Inselheim paused for a moment to weigh up his next question.

"Why did you bring me here?" he asked.

"To set you free, Mr. Inselheim."

Inselheim looked on, bewildered. *What is this guy talking about?*

"Do you like the room?" asked Stirner, turning his attention to their surroundings. "It's one of the nicer bedchambers in this mansion. It belonged once to a prince of the House Of Bourbon."

So there it was. Inselheim was in a mansion, likely in France. Until now he had no idea where he was. While blindfolded, he had imagined his destination to be an underground torture chamber or an open grave in the middle of nowhere. He had begun sweating profusely and shivering with fright once the van finally stopped and the engine turned off. They carried him out and up a flight of stairs, then untied him and left, locking the door behind them. He waited for a long time in silence before removing the blindfold. To his astonishment, he found himself inside an enormous bedroom with a lofty ceiling, patterned wallpaper, gold-framed paintings, a silver chandelier hanging in the middle and other lavish features. After inspecting his boarded-up luxury prison cell, he went through the inside door to find a marble bathroom, complete with spa.

"Breakfast is ready outside," said Stirner, half turning toward the door. "You must be anxious to stretch your legs and get some fresh air."

Inselheim hesitated. Was the tempting offer meant to lead him more easily into a trap? No, if they wanted to hurt or kill him, they would have already.

"Come. I'll explain everything," said Stirner. "It's a beautiful morning outside."

Inselheim reluctantly shifted across the bed and got to his feet. He inspected his attire, which he had found neatly folded on his bed when he first came. Then he looked up at Stirner. They were wearing matching outfits; chinos and a polo shirt. Stirner lifted his eyebrows expectantly. Inselheim walked forward slowly, and they left the room together.

The Impressionist paintings in the wide hallway were gigantic. The red carpet below Inselheim's feet was thick and plush. They descended the spiral stairway to the marble-tiled lobby, where the front door was wide open.

"This way," said Stirner, moving into the sunshine coming through the doorway.

Inselheim emerged onto the porch. The mansion was sitting on multiple acres of vibrant, perfectly manicured grass, bordered in the far distance by pine trees. With the bright blue sky for a backdrop, it was an impressive sight. The lavishness and size of the estate made Inselheim's place in Dahlem look like a summer cabin.

Stirner had already taken his seat at the head of the table. Spread out in front of him were platters of cheese and salami, coffee and milk, freshly cut fruit, sliced baguette, butter, wholegrain bread, multiple varieties of juice as well as croissants and macarons. Inselheim's place had been set at Stirner's right hand.

Inselheim turned and lifted his head to the sky and took a deep breath of the fresh country air.

"Lovely, isn't it?" said Stirner. "Kalakia prefers to spend his time in soulless penthouses and gloomy warehouses. He envies cultured men like you and me."

"If you and Kalakia are so different, why did you work for him?" said Inselheim, taking his place at the table.

"I didn't work *for* him," said Stirner. "He needed me to legitimise his power in Europe. Without me, he would be another mob boss peddling drugs and running prostitution rings."

"And you helped him out of the goodness of your heart?"

Stirner sighed and shook his head.

"He had undeniable strength and support, enough to weaken the global order. Once he consolidated world power under his banner, all that was left was for me to snatch it from him. That was my plan all along. He was a stepping stone, nothing more."

"To what?"

"To this moment. Here. Now. The League Of Reckoning is close to collapse. A new power is emerging, Mr. Inselheim, and you are at the heart of it."

Inselheim lifted his chin and stared earnestly at Stirner.

"My allies and I represent the rightful world order," said Stirner. "Kalakia thought he could put an end to the global hierarchy with his Robin Hood nonsense." Stirner snickered. "The League Of Reckoning is facing a reckoning of its own. Their ideology goes against human nature. Humans have an inherent need to know their rightful place. The world is always going to have masters who are superior to the rest, and we are going to remind Kalakia of his place soon enough."

"What are you going to do?"

"I have something special in mind," said Stirner, squinting and looking at the ground.

The two of them sat in silence for a moment. Inselheim's stomach began grumbling. They had fed him well while he was locked up in the room, but he had eaten nothing all morning. He took a croissant and began chewing on it while watching Stirner, whose mind had drifted elsewhere. Suddenly Stirner shook back to life. He gave Inselheim another dry smile.

"You must be eager to know why I brought you here," said Stirner.

"Of course," said Inselheim.

"I'll be honest with you, Mr. Inselheim. The coming year is going to be a volatile one for the inhabitants of this planet. Crushing The League and freeing the population is going to bring with it collateral damage. No part of the world will be immune. Millions of people might die, and the global economy will come to its knees."

Inselheim stopped chewing on his croissant and put it down on his plate.

"Excuse me? Did you say millions?"

"Well, not from any fault of mine. I hope to avoid needless suffering, but I know Kalakia. He doesn't care for human life. Just look at the vicious animals working for him. A recent killing by one of his people was utterly indescribable, I must tell you. The authorities counted dozens of stab wounds in one of the bodies. Dozens! Close to forty, if I'm not mistaken. That is pure insanity, wouldn't you agree?"

Inselheim sat there, dumbfounded.

"Considering the hostile environment Kalakia has created for innovative men such as yourself, what you and the Neutralaser team achieved was nothing short of miraculous," said Stirner, not skipping a beat. "And Kalakia wanted to shelve it. Your life's work. How did that make you feel?"

Inselheim's head felt suddenly hazy. He looked back on the past weeks and months. He grew tense when Vidrik entered his mind and he felt a terrible ache in his stomach.

"I wanted them all to die," he said, as an ominous feeling came down on him.

Stirner nodded approvingly.

"I understand completely," he said. "How long could we have survived with the spectre of nuclear war hanging over us? Rogue nations are pursuing arms. Conflict is inevitable. And the stakes are getting higher each day — not to mention all those close calls we've had. The Cuban Missile Crisis. Goldsboro. The Norwegian Incident. How many lives does this Earth have? You were right to develop the Neutralaser.

Without it, the world is coming to a horrific end. It is inevitable, isn't it?"

"Right," said Inselheim. "My father told me the same thing. Only pure luck helped us avoid catastrophe so far."

"Your father understood not only how crucial armament was for survival, but also how advances in weaponry could save lives, rather than taking them. He was a wise man."

"He was," said Inselheim quietly, lowering his head.

"The era of nation-states is over. Nations are impotent when it comes to global problems. They are doomed to fall into conflict. We need to evolve to the next level of civilisation; otherwise it's over for us."

Inselheim knew what Stirner was getting at, and it terrified him. But he could not help agreeing. The world had irreversibly changed since the inception and rise of The League Of Reckoning, and there was no going back from it.

"What if I told you that you could still develop the Neutralaser?" said Stirner. Inselheim suddenly left his thoughts behind and perked up. "What if your dream could still become a reality?"

"What do you mean?" said Inselheim with a quiet voice, seduced by the idea.

"I want to fund the mass-production of the Neutralaser. Ground-based and satellite. I'll provide you with a place from which to work and all the resources you need."

Inselheim felt unsettled by Stirner's generous offer, and immediately began to scrutinise it. Was Stirner messing with him? If not, what did he have planned for the Neutralaser?

"Don't just hear it from me," said Stirner. "There's someone here you should talk it over with."

Stirner looked over Inselheim's shoulder. Inselheim turned around, and his jaw went slack. Brunswick was walking toward him from the door like in a dream. He rose slowly from his chair in a state of numb disbelief.

"Kimberley?"

"Michael," said Brunswick as she embraced him.

"Take your time," said Stirner, getting up and walking away.

Inselheim finished hugging Brunswick then cupped her cheek with his hand, his face softening at the sight of her. She rubbed his arm in return.

"I'm so glad to see you," said Inselheim.

"How are you?" she said.

"Much better now," said Inselheim. "Are you ok?"

"Yes, they've taken care of us," said Brunswick.

Inselheim searched around and noticed they were alone. Brunswick locked her arm around his, and they walked together out to the yard, the grass plush beneath their feet. The sun and open space now felt rejuvenating to Inselheim, but only because of Brunswick's sudden appearance. Before that he could barely sense it. He looked at her again to confirm that she was real. They walked in silence, and Inselheim enjoyed the brief reprieve from the nightmare that had become his life. Having Brunswick there was like getting a shot of the most magnificent drug in the world. The effect would wear off eventually, but for the time being it was good to have her.

"The team?" said Inselheim.

"They're holding up, considering the situation. I'm proud of them."

"I can't wait to see them," said Inselheim.

Neither Brunswick nor Inselheim mentioned Aiko, Lena or Jonas, or Marius and the other five who The League had

80

brutally killed, but the long, sudden lull acted as a sombre reminder.

"Where are they keeping you?" asked Inselheim.

"In the most luxurious prison you can imagine. We're upstairs."

"I can imagine it. I've been upstairs as well."

"Really?"

Inselheim nodded and smiled.

"It's a relief to have access to showers and fresh clothes," said Brunswick.

"How did they find you?" said Inselheim.

"That's the thing," said Brunswick. "I called in, and Anke Müller got in touch with our contacts at NATO. These guys showed up in their place."

"Strange," said Inselheim. "Do you think she sold out?"

"Possibly. I would have done the same thing in her position."

"What did they tell you so far?"

"About what they want?"

"Yes."

"They want us to mass-produce the Neutralaser," said Brunswick.

"They told me the same thing."

"We're not here for our charm."

Inselheim stopped walking and fell to the grass. Brunswick sat beside him and stretched her legs out. She had on a white t-shirt and loose-fitting black pants. Her hair, tied into a bun, looked dry and brittle. She had developed wrinkles beneath her eyes. Inselheim was in no better shape. He knew he had lost weight, and that he had grown more greys. Recent events had left them both showing the signs of long-term stress.

"I don't know if I trust this Stirner guy," said Inselheim.

"He's not to be trusted. This is all an act," said Brunswick.

"So what do we do?"

"We have to make the most of the situation. Besides, if we don't play along, they'll kill us all."

"Suppose we do play along," said Inselheim. "It could open the gates of hell if these guys get a monopoly over the Neutralaser. The point of the technology is to nullify nuclear weapons. It's not supposed to be a tool for tyranny."

"We knew the risks when we started," said Brunswick. "Plus Kalakia already has the blueprints. The tyrant has what he wants. We can't stop now."

"So you think we should do this?"

Inselheim realised that Brunswick had been running her tongue side to side over her bottom lip for some time, the way she did when she was dissecting the situation and analysing every possibility. She remained thinking while staring at the grass, appearing able to see deep underground. The ferocity in her eyes when she turned back to Inselheim caused him to flinch.

"Yes," said Brunswick. "We're going to finish what we started."

"And if Stirner has something sinister in mind?"

"You're underestimating us again, Michael," said Brunswick, suddenly rising to her feet and brushing the blades of grass off her behind while looking toward the mansion. "This could be the chance of a lifetime."

Inselheim had not noticed, but Stirner was now walking toward them.

"And?" said Stirner as he approached.

"You've got a deal, Mr. Stirner," said Brunswick, reaching her hand out.

"Call me Horst," said Stirner, shaking her hand and grimacing when he noticed how firm her grip was.

Inselheim knew that look. Brunswick's tiny frame always put powerful men at ease until they shook hands with her. The situation troubled Inselheim, but he also felt a tinge of new life moving around inside him. They were in a terrifying situation with a dangerous new partner, but at least he and Brunswick were back together. It was enough to reassure him, to give him the faintest hope that he could still actualise his father's life-long dream — and come out of it all alive.

10

"I can't believe I wasn't going to come today," said Chi.

Ida picked up her bag with her martial arts uniform inside.

"You know when you're lying there on the sofa, all tired and lazy," continued Chi while folding her pants. "And then a voice in your head tells you don't bother going to martial arts class, just stay home?"

"Oh, yes," said Ida. "That voice is the devil."

"I know. Once you get into a flow it's like 'why did I ever think that?' I feel so pumped right now! I could fight anybody."

Chi gave Ida a nudge.

"Let's go. Me and you," said Chi, getting into fight stance and grinning.

Ida remained cool, pursing her lips and lifting her head. Her and Chi were the last two people in the changing rooms.

"I'm a lover, not a fighter," she said, exaggerating her Spanish accent, which had faded since she moved abroad.

Chi lowered her arms and tilted her head.

"Really? Every time a lover boy shows up, you fight him off."

Ida felt a sudden sharp ache in her chest.

"That's not true," she said.

"Aha, whatever you say," said Chi with a shrug.

"It's not," said Ida, raising her voice, her cheeks quickly warming up. She pushed Chi in the shoulder.

"Oh, so now she wants to fight!"

Ida pinched her lips tight. What did Chi mean exactly?

"Come on, lover girl," said Chi, throwing her bag over her shoulder and chuckling to herself as she walked to the exit.

The two of them thanked their sensei and left the dojo, coming out onto the bustle of Karl-Marx-Strasse, where Ida's bad mood followed. Chi was playfully trying to tell her something. All of the girls had made off-handed comments in the past, but for some reason it stuck this time. Ida had assumed her attitude toward men was a natural reaction to the past few months. She had seen more than enough death for a lifetime, and had begun to wake up feeling cold and empty. During the daytime she had stopped noticing the small details around her. Her sense of smell had faded. Now Chi was suggesting that she had turned away from love. They walked among a swarm of people, with Ida pondering what effect the world's ugliness was having on her.

"Did you see the news this morning?" said Chi. "Those murders in Poznan?"

"Yes," replied Ida, coming out of her thoughts. "I couldn't keep reading. It was terrible."

"There were children in that building. How could any-body mutilate somebody like that in public? Do you think it has anything to do with what people talk about on the inter-net? That secret organisation which exists but doesn't exist?"

"I don't know," said Ida while an uneasy feeling seeped in.

"Ida?" came a woman's voice cutting through the crowd from behind.

Ida and Chi slowed down and turned in unison to find the lady from the flea market, who had halted her walk and had her body half turned. She looked stunning, Ida noticed, wearing a cream-coloured designer coat, a white blouse with no bra, black satin trousers and black stilettos. Her make-up was flawless, her shade of lipstick complimenting her face perfectly. She did not belong in Neukölln, where most people stuck with tattered vintage clothing and black streetwear and sneakers.

"Hi," stuttered Ida, blinking rapidly. "I'm sorry, I don't think I remember your name."

The woman smiled and turned to face her.

"I don't think I told you my name. I'm Tina," she said, leaning forward and offering her hand. Her grip was firm.

"Nice to meet you," said Ida. She then turned to Chi. "This is my friend Chi," she added.

"Yes, I remember you from the market. Nice to meet you, Chi," said Tina in a professional manner while shaking Chi's hand.

"Likewise," said Chi after a short hesitation.

Tina smiled warmly at Chi then turned back to Ida.

"It's funny I run into you just before I fly back to Paris. I was thinking about you this morning. Those friends I told about you, I showed one of them your work. He loved it. He's actually a scout for the major labels, and he thinks you've got some potential. If you... I know this is out of the blue, but would you be interested in meeting him this week?"

"Uh," said Ida, shrugging and turning toward Chi. "I don't know."

Chi said nothing, only stared back at Ida with a blank expression.

"I know it's unexpected, but he was genuinely impressed. Anyway, he'll be in Paris with me for the week before I have to go back to Stockholm. Here." Tina took a business card out of her pocket and handed it to Ida. "Think about it and let me know. We can fly you out and cover your expenses. I don't think it would hurt to listen to what he has to say. Could be a great opportunity to learn about the industry."

"Ok," said Ida, wide-eyed. "I'll think about it and let you know."

"Great," said Tina with a nod and a smile. "It was nice to see you. Chi, a pleasure to meet you too."

Tina shook hands with Ida and Chi then marched away down the street, catching numerous glances from the Berliners around her.

Ida turned to Chi with a slack mouth. Someone from the fashion industry wanted to speak to *her*?

"You're not going, are you?" said Chi abruptly.

"What?" said Ida, tilting her head. "You don't think I should go?"

"People like her are one of the reasons I wanted to leave the States. All they care about is money. Those soulless companies bait you with success, then they suck you dry. It's ugly."

Ida crossed her arms and shifted her weight to her other leg.

"That's business, no?" she said.

"I don't trust her," said Chi.

"Why not?" said Ida as her pulse quickened.

"Because I don't. You're better than those people. And I've seen too many of my friends get hurt."

Ida's jaw grew tense.

"I can take care of myself, you know?" she said.

Chi sighed and looked away down the street.

"You're going to regret it," she said. "You're on a good thing already. You should stick with it instead of looking for shortcuts."

Chi was getting on Ida's nerves. *Who does she think she is?*

"Why are you being like this?" said Ida.

"Like what?" said Chi. "Also, don't you have work at the cafe tomorrow and Friday?"

"I'll tell them I can't come in. I can't pass up this opportunity."

"If you say so," said Chi.

Ida could not bear to hear anymore.

"Look, I need to go," she said. "I forgot I have to pick up my jacket from the dry cleaner. I'll see you later."

Ida stormed off, immediately getting caught behind a group of three people sauntering side by side and blocking the footpath. She moved to the edge of the gutter and forced her way around, grunting as she brushed a man on the way past. She stomped forward without a destination, embarrassed by her retreat but also infuriated with Chi. Ida never thought Chi would be the jealous type. *I guess you never really know people*, she figured, speeding up her march to nowhere.

Frederich shoved his wet pants and underwear into his bag and tossed it onto the back seat. He stood out in the open for a moment, his head freezing over and goosebumps covering his arms from the breeze. The thought hit him to check in with Intel. He got into the driver's seat and picked up his phone.

"Abel," said Gerricks immediately upon answering.

"Gerricks."

"What's your status?"

"I'm still in Poland. I needed to take a short detour."

"You still haven't made it out of the country? Do you know the shit storm you created?"

"I blacked out."

"You what? Shit. Ok, listen. The Polish police know you're with us. They won't give you trouble. They're glad the Berlin bomber's dead, but they're pissed about the mess you left behind. But whatever, it's what Scheffler wanted. I probably don't need to tell you how happy he is with your work."

"What's the media saying?" asked Frederich.

"Nothing yet. They know what to report. Vigilante killing. Nobody's going to grieve when they find out Drexler was the one you hacked up."

"Ok," said Frederich, numb to the significance of Gerricks' words.

"Also, we need you to get to London straight away. We're pushing forward with the counter-assault in two days," said Gerricks. "I've got the brief for your next mission. We want you to take out five marks in one go. Can you handle that many?"

"Send it through," said Frederich.

"Roger that. There's a jet waiting in Brandenburg to take you straight there."

"Ok."

"Need anything in the meantime?"

"No, I'm fine."

"Good luck," said Gerricks and hung up.

Frederich turned the car on and put it into gear. No point brooding about what happened in Poznan, he thought. Drexler got what was coming to him. It would be better for

Frederich to focus his energy on his new mission. *Next time just keep it together.*

He pulled out onto the road and sped off, figuring he should tank up soon. A short while later, he turned his head and listened carefully to the constant wail behind him. He checked his rearview mirror and saw the blinking lights. The sound of the siren grew louder. *Police.* Gerricks said they understood the situation? There was no one around beside Frederich. The sirens were definitely for him. The police car raced toward him from behind before switching lanes and driving alongside him. The police officer behind the wheel, a fresh-faced young man with a prominent jawline, signalled for Frederich to pull over. Frederich continued along for a while, thinking hard, before finally planting his foot on the accelerator. Plan A would be to outrun him. Something in the guy's eyes was unsettling. Why had he come after Frederich alone?

A small gap opened between them when Frederich sped up, which the rogue policeman quickly reeled in. Frederich's three cylinders were not going to be enough to outrun the police car, especially in open country. He followed the road with the policeman inches behind him, the siren still blaring. The trail ended ahead at a T-intersection, and Frederich spun the wheel right without slowing down, shooting across the dirt before returning to the bitumen. He learnt his first lesson about his pursuer; he was not a skilled driver. The policeman's back wheels spun out of control while trying to emulate Frederich's turn, which forced him to a stand-still. He made up the distance quickly, and they were back where they had begun, the police car's nose right on Frederich's tail. Frederich looked to his passenger seat and caught a glimpse of Plan B; his pistol. He knew he would win a shoot-out.

No doubt about it. He would bet his life on it. *Don't*, came Kraas' voice. *No killing police officers.* Frederich agreed that he had to draw the line somewhere. Kraas was a firm believer in respecting members of the law, except in cases of corruption. Frederich was in the wrong after what he had done; according to the law, at least.

The policeman pulled up level in the opposite lane. Without warning, he steered toward Frederich's car. Frederich reacted quickly, jerking his wheel to get out of the way, half of his car going onto the dirt. He veered back onto the road, wondering if he should make an exception for his no killing cops rule. He looked through the police car's window and saw the policeman furiously yelling in his direction. The guy was unhinged. It was time to get creative. Frederich slammed the brakes and turned the wheel at the same time. The movies had made it look easy. In Frederich's case he spun terribly out of control onto the grass, his car coming close to tipping over. His heart was revving as quickly as the engine.

He took a deep breath and slammed the accelerator again. He was already on the grass, so he continued off-road. His wheels spun in place before his car jerked forward. All he saw at first in the rearview mirror was mud flying in the air, before the police car appeared again and followed him onto the field. To his right was a long fence with a herd of cows on the other side, to his left was a forest in the far distance. He went left. *What's the plan?* He had opened up another gap, which meant he had a short time window to get himself into position. He pulled up with his car parallel to the forest and the driver's side facing the trees. He grasped his pistol and forced the door open, flicked off the safety and pointed the gun in the direction of the approaching police car. *No more games.* This guy was going to learn to behave himself, or he was going to get a bullet in the skull.

The police car pulled up twenty feet away. Frederich waited. His engine crackled from the heat, his breath was shallow and quick. There was no sign of movement ahead. The glare of the sun on the police car's windshield blocked Frederich's sight. After a long pause, the driver's door flung open. The policeman got out and emerged into the open, pointing his pistol forward with both hands. *Brave man.* He was small-statured with straight posture you only see in the military or the police.

"Put the gun down, you bastard!" he screamed.

Frederich knew that if he was going to shoot, he had best do it immediately. He tightened his finger around the trigger.

"Do you know what you did!?" screamed the policeman. His face was flushed bright red, his eyes forced unnaturally open. Frederich could see the whites from where he was. "There were children there! What kind of animal are you?"

A wave of lightheadedness hit Frederich and spun his head backwards. His grip around the pistol began to loosen involuntarily. *Children?* He remembered the woman who entered the building with her two boys. He had barely given them a second thought. Had they seen something?

"You call yourselves honourable?" the policeman continued. "Is that what justice looks like?"

Frederich's mind turned blank. He hesitated for a long time while the pistol grew heavy in his hand. Finally, he let it go, leaving it on the roof and emerging from behind the car empty-handed. The policeman ran forward quickly and pressed the barrel of his gun against Frederich's chest. Frederich could feel the policeman's hands shaking with fury. He kept his arms at his side and remained calm. Too calm. He felt something leave him, and in its place the shadow descended on him like a thick fog.

"What about the children?" he said.

The policeman hesitated.

"What happened after I left?" said Frederich.

"The tear gas," said the policeman. "The family on the floor above believed it was a fire. They ran down the stairs. To escape. They saw…" The policeman faltered. His lips began trembling, his eyes filled with tears. His arms were shaking uncontrollably.

Frederich did not need to hear the rest. He pushed his chest into the barrel of the gun and looked directly into the policeman's eyes.

"Shoot," he said. "End this now."

The policeman's eyes opened wider still, his mouth falling completely open. He looked as though he were staring directly into the gates of hell, witnessing a sight so horrible that he could not possibly fathom it. It was not hell, thought Frederich, but it was close.

"Pull the trigger," said Frederich. "You have to."

He closed his eyes and waited, focussed into the abyss and asked it to welcome him in. It was as good a time as any. He did not want to know anything more about what the policeman had experienced, or what those young boys had seen. Whatever happened, it was horrific, and he had caused it. He deserved this.

The barrel fell off his chest. He heard a sob, followed by a long silence, then another sob. He opened his eyes. The policeman was crouched down on the ground, the gun held limp at his side while he cried into the ground. He let out a long groan, then began screaming, lifting his head to the sky

94

with his voice booming across the field. Frederich watched on, not knowing what to do. The policeman's sobbing eventually settled into a soft whimper while he pressed his face into the dirt.

Frederich's hand reached out by itself to touch the man, before he turned suddenly and went back to his car. He snatched his pistol off the roof and got in and switched on the engine. The policeman had still not moved. Frederich put the car into gear and drove off without looking back.

11

Frederich had less than twenty-four hours to terminate five killers. Once the counter-offensive began, his targets would quickly figure out what was going on, and he would lose his opportunity. The only options were to get it done all at once, or pick off his targets one-by-one without leaving a mess. If he acted too hastily before the deadline, he could compromise the whole plan.

Bibby, Dikka, Pistol, Faust and Vent were their nicknames. Frederich had no idea what their actual names were, no clue at all who they were. Whether they had family, wives or children, it mattered little. He could not have cared less about what kind of music they enjoyed or what their favourite cuisine was. He only knew they had to go. According to the report from Gerricks, they were members of a hit squad which killed six League soldiers and injured three others. That was all the reason Frederich needed. Attached to the brief were even pictures of their attack, taken from a low position beside the street. Likely a hidden camera in a storm drain.

Bibby was monstrous in size, a beefcake with a fat neck and small head. Dikka was a skinhead with a psychopathic stare. Pistol looked too pretty to be part of such a vicious crew. Faust was German for fist. Probably a boxer, judging by his nickname, sturdy appearance and crooked nose. The only photo of Vent was a police mugshot of an anorexic looking man with a potent stare. He was nowhere to be seen in the attack pictures.

The London borough of Bromley where the five men all lived had a small-town feel. Frederich had spent the flight over carefully studying the map. Kraas always insisted that geography was crucial in the art of war. There would be no time for second-guessing when the time came. If things escalated quickly or went wrong, Frederich would need to know the area if he was to use it to his advantage. It was for this reason that he spent the morning walking through the sleepy neighbourhood, passing by each of the homes of his targets, noting the connecting streets along with places of interest such as parks or alleyways. There was no need for photos, partly because they would draw unwanted attention, mostly because Frederich trusted his memory. Later that afternoon, when he had seen enough, he decided to drop into the local pub for a beer.

The 'Stern and Dolly' was a light brown building which stood at the head of two intersecting streets on a backdrop of grey clouds. Two construction workers sat at the front drinking their beers on a bench beneath an outdoor umbrella compliments of the 'Berett' brewery. The pair were still dressed in their paint-speck-covered work shorts and steel-capped boots. They paused their conversation and gawked at Frederich as he approached the entrance, dressed in a black t-shirt and black jeans and his hair in a knotty mess. He wondered how he smelt, his only shower being that bath in the lake. Probably not great.

He stepped inside and immediately counted five people, including the bartender. On the outside the place looked decent enough, the interior on the other hand was rougher than he expected. The bar was at the back, fitted with over a dozen gold-coloured beer taps and a dark, stained-oak bench lined with black stools. Behind the bar were dozens of bottles of spirits and liqueurs. The surrounding area had a variety of old, randomly grouped, single and double seater leather couches which were worn and ripped all over. In the middle was a brick-pillar supporting a round standing-only table. Frederich spotted the word 'pisser' etched into the side of the wood. There was an exit door behind the bar and an opening covered in old stickers which led to the toilets. It was early in the week, so Frederich did not imagine the place getting too crowded in the evenings. According to the brief from Intel, the Stern and Dolly was where his targets met for a drink almost every night. There were two evenings to go before the assault began. Frederich would wait for them to come to the pub and leave, hopefully intoxicated, then he would strike. Anyone who did not show up would get a home visit instead.

"Can I help you?" said the bartender, a bald, middle-aged man with black-rimmed glasses.

"Yes," said Frederich. "I'd like a pint of beer, and a bowl of nuts, if you have them."

The bartender turned to one of his customers at the far end of the bar.

"Right, well, take a seat instead of just standing there," said the bartender. "You're making old David here nervous."

"Only one who makes me nervous around here is you, Liam," replied the man named David.

Liam the bartender snickered before turning back to Frederich and thrusting a small ashtray filled with salted peanuts in front of him.

"So what'll it be? A pint of what?" he asked with his hands on the bar, signalling toward the beer taps with his head.

"I'll have a stout," said Frederich, taking a seat on the barstool.

"Coming right up," said Liam after maintaining an abnormal amount of eye contact.

Liam fetched a glass and went over to the beer tap. Then came the question Frederich was expecting.

"So where you from?" said Liam, holding the glass at an angle while pouring the beer.

"Germany," said Frederich. "Small town in the East."

Liam looked up at Frederich with a curious expression.

"Germany?"

"That's right," said Frederich.

"What brings you to Bromley?"

"Visiting friends for a bachelor party this weekend."

"Aha," said Liam, wiping the excess head of foam from the glass and topping it up. "So you've got more friends in this town than old Dave over here."

"I'm about to have one less friend if you don't watch yourself," yelled David from the other side of the bar while cradling his glass of beer.

Liam handed the beer over to Frederich, who took his first sip.

"Hope it suits your German taste?"

"It's great," replied Frederich.

"Glad to hear," said Liam.

Frederich remained at the bar sipping his beer and eating his peanuts while Liam disappeared out back. Frederich and David exchanged the odd glance, but neither of them spoke. A group of three guys in t-shirts and jeans sat in the corner on the other side of the pub chatting and randomly breaking out into laughter. Frederich spent the time inspecting the place more closely. It had seen better days. Years of rough use had left marks and scratches all over the tables. The carpet was heavily worn in places, revealing the concrete beneath. One large section was charred-out, probably from an accidental fire. Frederich was thinking about going to the bathroom before Liam returned with a cask of beer.

"So how long have you had this place?" asked Frederich.

"Too long," said Liam, placing the cask on the floor in the corner. "Since before you were born."

Frederich nodded approvingly.

"You must have seen a lot in that time."

"Oh, yes," said Liam. "We get some interesting people coming in here."

"Is that right?"

"He means interesting criminals," yelled David from his position.

"Don't talk about yourself that way, Dave," yelled back Liam with a turn of the head before bringing his attention back to Frederich. "Things get rowdy in here during the evenings."

"I like rowdy," said Frederich.

"I don't think it's for you, no disrespect," said Liam. "Our customers don't play nicely with outsiders. You're better off just coming during the day. Like David."

"That's right, kiddo," said David. "Enjoy yourself a quiet beer then go home."

"These must be some serious guys," said Frederich.

"Oh, yes," said Liam. "But they usually keep the trouble outside, which is lucky for me."

"When do they come?" asked Frederich. "So I know when I shouldn't be here."

"Usually after 9."

"Good to know," said Frederich.

"Don't let it sour your visit, though," said Liam. "These guys are the exception, not the rule."

"I'm a big fan of this city," said Frederich. "Good beer, good people." He finished his glass off and stood up. "Thanks."

"Oh look, now you scared him off," yelled out David.

Frederich dropped a ten-pound note on the bar.

"I'll see you next time," he said. "Early, of course."

Liam took the note and gave Frederich his change.

"Pleasure," he said with a straight face. "Catch you next time."

Frederich took a final look around then left the bar, feeling satisfied and ready to find a motel he could nap in. *Nice guys*, he thought as he walked down the street — *and incredibly helpful.*

Ida bit on her nails while standing in the queue at Tegel Airport, eagerly awaiting her flight to Paris. She adjusted her shirt for the hundredth time, making sure she had it evenly tucked into her trousers. She ran through the details of Tina's email in her head, including their upcoming meeting and the cocktail party. *Cocktail party.* Hearing those words from Tina gave Ida a wonderful feeling. Ida loved nothing more than a reason to dress up, a chance she barely got in a city like Berlin. It numbed her mind even to imagine attending such an event with someone linked to the major fashion labels. She pictured all the beautiful, immaculately dressed women who would be there with their long legs and curvy bodies. She cursed herself for only packing her blue dress.

102

She also had a short, strapless red dress, but she had not wanted to stand out too much. It would have been smarter to pack both and decide which one to wear when she got to the hotel. There had been no time to think of such things. Her mind overran with frantic thoughts from the moment she called Tina that evening. Before she knew it, she had cancelled her work shifts at the cafe and agreed to a next day flight. The email came through an hour later; accommodation at a five-star hotel near the Champs-Élysées, a meeting the following morning in the business district, after which there would be a rooftop party that evening.

The argument with Chi crossed Ida's mind but she quickly pushed the thought away. The tight spaces and bland architecture at Tegel Airport made her even more impatient to get in the air. The queue eventually got moving and she reached the counter, presenting her phone to the scanner to have her boarding pass approved. The light on the device turned green, and the hostess smiled politely and thanked her. Any doubts Ida had that the whole thing was a joke were dispelled with the validation of her ticket. She still had her feet firmly on the ground in Berlin, far away from the bustle of Paris. The moment she crossed that barrier, she would be in new territory, and that terrified her. It was also exhilarating. Her stomach was doing funny things, churning and rolling around without her permission. The inside of her chest was ready to burst out and board the plane without her. She smiled with wide-eyes at the hostess and walked through, tucking her phone into her pocket. Outside on the tarmac it was already dark, with the jet patiently waiting to receive passengers and leave. *I'm not ready for this*, she thought, then told herself that life did not care about readiness. Things like parenthood, new careers, travelling to the other side of the world — who was ever ready for such things? She had to embrace the point of no return. She was heading to Paris to pursue the next phase of her dreams, and she was determined to make the most of it. She marched forward and slowly entered the plane behind the rest of the people, putting her bag in the overhead compartment and buckling up before resuming biting her nails as the pilot gave the greeting announcement and the flight attendants made the final preparations.

12

The series of computer screens showed footage of the cities and territories under Scheffler's control. Europe was crawling with The League's spies and scouts, all backed by an extensive web of soldiers and assassins ready to reign down justice. Some civilians strolled by along the streets casually chatting, others had their attention on their smartphones while they walked. One man with glasses stood at the corner talking on his phone while pacing from side to side. All of them were oblivious to the conflict brewing beneath the facade of ignorance they called everyday life. The continent would soon become a battlefield, and as the war heated up, the people would be forced to reckon with harsh reality. Meanwhile, Scheffler was stuck in a bunker, far away from the action. It felt wrong. He had risen the ranks because he could perform under high pressure. How was he supposed to coordinate the war without the fear and sweat of being in the field?

Gerricks was busy flicking through an endless series of scout reports. Unlike Scheffler, he was where he belonged. He had a brain bigger than Scheffler's biceps. Scheffler mindlessly inspected his arm. *Damn.* He was already losing size since tapering off the steroids. How long had he been General? Two weeks? His throat suddenly felt thick and the room shrunk around him. He left abruptly and went into his office and shut the door behind him, got down to the ground and started doing push-ups. His joints ached straight away, as fatigue hit and the consequences of cutting out his steroid cycles impacted his performance. *Come on.* He had just completed fifty reps when his arms gave out. He rolled to his side and began panting, feeling nauseous and out of breath. A month earlier he could do over a hundred without breaking a sweat. Maybe he was not made for this General business. How would his men ever respect a weakling? He needed to get back in the line of danger, had to get his edge back.

There was a loud knock on the door.

"What?" he yelled out, rising to his feet.

Gerricks came in and paused in the doorway, looking hesitantly at the sweat-covered, out-of-breath Scheffler.

"What is it?" said Scheffler impatiently.

"Something came up in the scout reports," said Gerricks, pushing the dreadlocks out of his face. "Do you want to come see?"

Scheffler nodded and followed Gerricks into the surveillance room.

"In Barcelona we're tracking forty-three targets from the Five Eyes list," said Gerricks as he returned to his workstation.

"Right," said Scheffler.

"Well," said Gerricks, pointing to his computer screen. "Nineteen of them have paid a visit to this building in the last twenty-four hours."

Scheffler studied the live footage of a building with an orange sandstone facade.

"What do we know?" asked Scheffler.

"It's in El Raval. Nightlife district. There's an illegal brothel on the third level, so first we figured these guys were just going there for some action. But then we noticed something else. Pretty much all of them came in empty-handed then left with the same kind of backpack."

"What else?"

"That's it. It's a mystery."

Scheffler stared attentively at random people passing by along the narrow cobbled alleyway.

"What should we do?" asked Gerricks.

"Send in a scout," said Scheffler. "I want to know what's going on. They could be preparing for an attack."

"Might be risky. Should we be making incursions right now?"

"I said I want to know what's going on. Get someone in there. Tell them to be discreet."

"Ok," said Gerricks. "I'll make it happen."

"Good man," said Scheffler and slapped Gerricks' shoulder before marching out of the room.

Piotr Paleski dropped to his knees and rested his elbows on the bed in a steeple position, resting his forehead on his knuckles. He had no other choice left. It was either this or go insane.

"Lord," he whispered, closing his eyes. "Give me the strength to fight. The strength to make the right decisions. The strength to…" He paused and took a deep breath. "…to kill." He pushed his forehead harder into his knuckles. "Protect my family, spare them from what I have done and what I am about to do. Please, take their pain into your tender embrace, and shield them from the evil that is inside me. Amen."

He lifted his head and opened his eyes, relaxed his hands, then turned his head. On the bedside table sat a Makarov pistol; all-steel with a firm trigger — a heavy piece for its size. Beside it were the knuckle dusters; dark silver and extra chunky. The dusters would make the most impact without causing death, stunning his target long enough to be taken in without a fuss. The Makarov would solve any unexpected complications.

Ralph's snoring came through the paper-thin walls separating their motel rooms. It would be the two of them tomorrow. Piotr's first choice for a partner would not have been Ralph. He would be far more confident with Frederich by his side. Wishful thinking. He would need to make the best of what he had. His life depended on it. Anyway, what annoyed him more than Ralph's snoring was the guy's ability to fall asleep any time he pleased. Piotr had slept terribly since he was a child, often waking up in the middle of the night filled with anxiety and paranoia. Now he had an extra reason not to sleep. Something big was brewing, although the information coming out of Intel was scarce. All they had was a pair of photos and an address, and all they knew was they had to break into the guy's house at 3:00 am and take him alive, and not a minute sooner.

It was Piotr's first mission. If anything went wrong, it would also be his first kill. His paranoia was racing, as he pictured every worst-case scenario. He wondered how a gunshot would feel, how terrible the burn would be, or how loud his scream would become in response to the pain. Or rather how would he react if they went in and there were innocents in the same room? He pictured the man's young daughter, scared stiff by the intruder with the knuckle dusters intended for her father's face, her innocent mind unable to comprehend what was happening. What if the guy saw them coming and had his shotgu—

Screw this. Piotr snatched his room keys off the table and stormed out of the motel room, slamming the door shut behind him. His feet crunched over the gravel path beside the freeway as he charged toward the trees. He left behind the whooshing of the cars on the Autobahn and began his ascent, pushing hard up the hill while dodging the tree trunks in his way. His thighs burnt and his chest ached, but he continued his climb, determined to make it to the top. The hill eventually tapered out, and he made it to the peak. He gasped and panted, entirely out of breath, his whole body now throbbing from the strain and the lack of oxygen. With his hands on his hips he looked out over the terrain dotted with lights. The anxiety which had gripped him in the motel had eased, and his focus sharpened again. He hoped the physical exhaustion would be enough to help him sleep. His next chance would not come for another forty-eight hours.

If he survived that long.

Scheffler wrinkled his brow while rapidly tapping his finger on the desk.

"How long has it been?" he asked.

"Six hours," said Gerricks. "He was supposed to get out of there after twenty-minutes if he found nothing."

"Which means he found something."

"Seems so."

Scheffler rubbed his palm over his mouth. *Shit.*

"What should we do?" said Gerricks.

Storm the place, Scheffler thought to himself. *Storm the fucking place.*

109

"Keep your eyes peeled," he said and marched out.

When he got inside his office he slammed the door shut behind him and began pacing from side to side. He stopped beside his desk and clenched his fists. The urge to kick his chair over came but he held it back. His eyes were stinging from lack of sleep, and his head felt fuzzy. *Think, Vince, think.* His only real option was to wait. He had already taken an unnecessary risk by sending in the scout. Kalakia had been clear about staying put, and Scheffler had defied the order. The assault was beginning in less than twenty-four hours. He picked up his phone but stopped before dialling the number. How would he explain that he had screwed up? He put the phone down and began pacing again. Waiting was not his style. It made him feel frustrated. Impotent. He was the guy they called on to make things happen, not to wait for things to happen to him. Something was going on in that building. There was still a slim chance that he had made the right decision. What if his inaction had ended up costing lives? They could send in another scout, this time with more caution. Then Scheffler would call Kalakia, justified in his decision. He pushed the door open and returned to the surveillance room.

"Send someone else—"

The impact when he saw Gerricks' face was immediate, and he slowed his walk to a halt. Gerricks stared gravely at him with wide-eyes.

"What is it?" said Scheffler.

Gerricks turned to his terminal, which was showing an amateur video taken along the beachside. On the screen was a man's body hanging limp by its feet from a light pole. The police were cordoning off the area as shocked bystanders looked on. A police officer approached the camera before it was switched off.

"Who's that?" said Scheffler.

"That's our scout," said Gerricks. "They hung his body up at the main beach in Barcelona just before daylight. Someone uploaded the footage online."

13

Paris in the evening was breathtaking.

Gazing wide-eyed out of her taxi, Ida leaned forward and carefully studied every passing building and landmark. *Unreal.* Her second visit to the city was reminding her what picturesque meant. Driving along the Seine felt like being in a movie — a romantic one, of course. The grand buildings, the cobbled squares, the elegantly-dressed people; everything about the place was sublime.

They crossed Place de la Concorde and turned onto the Champs-Élysées, and Ida's senses began to prickle. She was lifted out of her body and had to grasp the edge of the seat. She was eight years old again, sitting on the carpet in front of her television watching a María Félix movie with her mother. Wrapped around María's neck was a baby blue silk scarf and in her hand was a cigarette. She had on a diamond-encrusted tiara and earrings, both of which sparkled and glowed as she spoke, each tilt of her head hypnotising the young Ida. The cigarette smoke lifting into the air had the effect of making María's wide, bright eyes look much more seductive, her uncompromising facial expression giving potency to her divine beauty. Ida remembered how she had ached to cross the screen and enter María's alluring world. Now only a car door separated her from the real thing.

The car came to a halt. Ida looked around abruptly and realised they had already turned off the Champs-Élysées and were now in the hotel driveway.

"Thank you," she muttered, before paying and getting out of the car.

The taxi driver walked around to the back and took her luggage bag out of the trunk. In a moment he was gone, and Ida was left standing in the middle of the driveway with her hand resting over the luggage handle.

Warm lighting illuminated the top of the arched windows at the entrance as well as the balconies above, and Ida moved toward the inviting glow. She was greeted at the front by the black tuxedo-clad doorman and then again inside the lobby. The receptionist was polite and softly-spoken. Before Ida knew it, her bag was on its way to her room and she was holding a room card. She left behind the shiny marble flooring, the low hanging chandeliers and the three shades of pink roses which surrounded the lobby, and took the lift up to the top level. Once inside, she found a luxuriant, king-sized bed awaiting her and noticed a hint of vanilla in the air. The room had full-body mirrors in various positions, gorgeous light-pink wallpaper and lush, white carpet. The attention to detail was worth admiring longer, but she crossed through the room and opened the door to the balcony instead. Her eyes lit up. The sparkling city landscape lay before her with the Eiffel Tower protruding magnificently out of the middle. A smile broke out on her face, and she hurried back inside to find some champagne to help her enjoy the moment.

Ida peered at the clock. 11:12 am. The meeting was at twelve, but no way she was leaving anything to chance. She picked up her handbag from the bed and began marching toward the door before realising she had left her room card on the dresser. *Slow down.* With the plastic card in her hand she paused and took a deep breath, then double-checked to make sure she had everything before leaving. The taxi was waiting for her outside and got her to La Défense twenty-five minutes early. The skyscrapers in the distance dwarfed her as she marched through the public square with her head lifted high. At 11:44 am she approached her destination; the Éclat Building on Rue de la Demi Lune.

The inside of the roughly thirty-storey building was crawling with business people in suits, and the surrounding area was enveloped by glass, with offices on all four sides having a view of the lobby through their floor-to-ceiling windows.

Ida had barely warmed her place on the leather couch in reception when she heard the sound of Tina's stilettos clacking through the lobby.

"Ida," said Tina with a smile as she approached. "You're early. I saw you come in from my office."

"Yes, I hope that's ok?" said Ida while standing up. "I can wait if you need more time."

"No, don't be silly," replied Tina, shaking Ida's hand. "Come. We're still one person short, but he'll be here soon. We can start without him."

Ida tucked her handbag close to her side and followed Tina across the lobby.

"Come, we'll take the stairs, it's just on the second level," said Tina. "Stretch our legs a bit."

Tina's office was an uninspiring space. It had a grey desk wedged against the window, a black leather sofa, a filing cabinet and a small round meeting table, along with a generic landscape painting hanging on the wall.

Tina sat first at the meeting table and began pouring two cups of sparkling water from the bottle sitting on a tray.

"So," said Tina after Ida had found a seat, pushing a cup in Ida's direction. "I'm glad you could make it."

"Oh, of course. Thank you for inviting me," said Ida.

Realising she was slouching Ida pushed her shoulders back and stuck her chest out slightly to correct her posture.

"Was the flight ok? The room?"

"Yes, everything's great. The hotel is amazing," said Ida.

"I'm glad you like it," said Tina, gazing into Ida's eyes for a long time.

Ida held eye contact for only a split second before feeling compelled to look away. When she turned her gaze back Tina was smiling, and Ida blushed. She wondered how nervous she looked.

Tina checked her watch then leaned back. *She's wearing a Cartier*, thought Ida. *How much is she earning?*

"So I showed my friend the sample of your work and the online store you set up. You walk a fine line, Ida. Every style choice you make theoretically shouldn't work. Nobody in the industry would even think about going there. But the way you bring each outfit together is almost genius. How do you do it?

Ida shrugged.

"I follow my feeling," she said, remembering the advice Chi gave her in Gorbachev's. "I try not to think too hard about it. I decide first, worry later. I guess I have nothing to lose doing it my way."

"No, that's right," said Tina while repeatedly nodding and with a look of fascination. "Well, that's the attitude we need. How did you come up with the name for your label?"

"It's not a label," said Ida.

"Not yet," said Tina, pulsating her eyebrows.

Ida's stomach fluttered at the thought, and she worked hard to push the feeling away. *Be professional.*

"I felt like the fashion industry focusses too hard on sex appeal," she began. "I mean, women should celebrate their sexuality, of course. But the feminist struggle is about so much more. I thought fashion should celebrate women's empowerment in other ways. So I called it the Virgin Queen Collection."

"Fascinating," said Tina. "Do you have any tips for how I could diversify the way I dress? To bring it more in line with your philosophy?"

"Oh, no," said Ida quickly, shaking her head. "No way. You always look beautiful. I like the way you mix business with sexiness."

"You think I'm sexy?" said Tina, pushing her eyebrows way up and giving Ida a sharp stare.

Ida giggled abruptly and blushed again.

"You know what I mean!" she blurted.

Tina chuckled. Her voice was measured and deep.

"Yes, I was only playing around," she said, before turning suddenly serious. "But if you want to be in this industry, don't ever forget; sex is a weapon. You don't go to war unarmed."

"What war?" said Ida.

"You'll see when the time comes," said Tina. "You'll get a glimpse tonight. I hope you brought something sexy with you for this evening? You only get one chance to make an impression."

"I have a dress, yes," said Ida. "I don't know how sexy it is."

Tina narrowed her gaze and looked Ida up and down. Then she reached into her handbag and took out a business card and handed it over.

"We can't take any risks," she said. "Here. Go to this store this afternoon and tell them I sent you."

"No, I can't," said Ida, holding her palm out.

"It's fine," said Tina. "Take it."

Ida reached out and reluctantly took the card.

"You have a wonderful body, Ida. Let's give it the outfit it deserves. I'm sure you can keep the Virgin Queen at home for one evening."

Ida gave a half-smile and looked down at the table then looked up again.

Tina checked her watch once more then took out her phone and tapped through it before frowning and shaking her head.

"Oh, that bastard, he always does this," she said. "He said he'll meet us at the party tonight. I'm sorry about this."

"Oh, ok," said Ida. "That's fine. It can wait."

"You get used to it," said Tina, giving Ida a reassuring smile. "So let's finish up. I'm sure you want time to relax and get yourself ready after you go shopping for your dress."

"Yes," said Ida, standing up simultaneously with Tina. "Thanks again for that."

"Of course," said Tina, shaking Ida's hand. "See you tonight."

"See you then," said Ida before pulling her handbag close and leaving the office.

Matthias Vidrik stood at the end of the hallway and watched Ida from behind as she walked toward the stairs. The sight of her caused his skin to prickle all over and his vision to scatter momentarily. *Patience. You'll have her soon.*

When Ida disappeared through the stairway exit he sauntered down the hallway and turned left to find Tina Radara perched on the edge of the table. She stared directly at him with that icy stare of hers before taking off her wig, revealing her shaved head. He took up a spot some distance from her.

"She's a charming a girl," said Radara. "I can see why you and Abel are so captivated by her."

"What's she wearing tonight?"

"That's a surprise."

"Mmm, I can't wait."

"I'm sure," said Radara. "Stay out of sight until it's time. I want her to myself first."

Vidrik curled his fingers and toes tightly.

"I understand the plan," he said with a raspy whisper.

"Good," said Radara sharply.

"If Stirner finds out what we're up to—"

"As long as you take care of Abel when the time comes, we'll be fine."

"Of course I will. And before he dies, he's going to know exactly what I have planned for her."

"I don't want to hear about your sick games," said Radara while looking away. "Your idea of fun is different to mine."

"At least I'm honest with my prey."

"What are you saying?" said Radara with a sudden venom in her voice, turning back toward Vidrik with her deathly stare. "That I'm dishonest?"

Vidrik snickered. *I could kill you right now, you cow.*

119

"Your approach has its uses," he said. "Even I can admit that."

"I'm glad," said Radara. "So show some appreciation. Without me, Ida would still be hanging around in some filthy Berlin dive bar, and you would have no way of getting to Abel. Without me you'd have nothing."

Vidrik sighed and lifted himself off the edge of the table.

"I'll be waiting downstairs for the two of you tonight," he said as he walked away. "Don't take too long."

Radara said nothing. Vidrik reached the doorway then turned around, finding her staring directly at him without a shred of emotion in her face. She remained motionless, not bothering to acknowledge that he was leaving. He froze, tormented by his inability to break through her walls. He was desperate to leave the room but her stare held him in place. The seconds ticked on, and still she remained, unflinching, inviting him to hate her even more. *What a disgusting...* She was so... so...

"Ah!" he finally yelled out in sheer frustration, slapping the air and forcing himself through the doorway before stomping his way through the corridor toward the stairs.

14

Ida carefully focussed on the reflection of her face in the mirror, inspecting every blemish that needed her attention. It was too quiet in the room for her liking, and she scoured around for the remote control and turned on the television. A French-dubbed Hollywood action movie which she had never seen appeared, and she flicked through the available channels until she found the English cable news.

"*Where is* Michael Inselheim?" said the presenter immediately. "The CEO of the Inselheim Group has been missing for over a week now after a break-in at his house, raising fears that he has been abducted. Concerns are growing for his safety, and a company spokesperson has made repeated calls for any information that could…"

They played old video footage of Inselheim at a business gathering as the presenter continued to speak. Ida shook her head disapprovingly. She had an idea what happened to him, but also had no intention of getting involved in that mess again.

Wearing the hotel robe over her dress to guard it against smudges, she got to work on her makeup while the television continued in the background. She put on moisturiser first followed by the primer. The foundation evenly spread, she picked up the concealer bottle and went about dabbing beneath her eyes before spreading the formula out with a sponge. Makeup done, eyelashes evenly spread and cheeks blushed, she grasped her lipstick and began painting her lips plum. She paused suddenly and moved her hand away while turning to the television. Two words had forced her to take notice of the current story. She watched as the newscaster re-capped the details of the gruesome killings in Poland, then turned stiff when the victim was revealed to be the Berlin Bomber. *Frederich.* Hours after he had come to see her, he was brutally murdering someone. *Thirty stab wounds.* Her hands grew clammy. She was taken back to their conversa-tion at Lustgarten when she first found out about him join-ing The League. How had he described himself? 'Not normal?' *I belong there*, he had said. Her affection for him was already hanging by a thread. What would cause him to act like that, she wondered? Only a monster could do such a thing. Frederich was not... or was he? She blinked hard and shook her head before mindlessly turning back to the mirror to finish what she was doing.

Within minutes she picked up her phone and handbag and rushed out of the door in a lightheaded state. The taxi ride to the Éclat Building turned into a complete blur. She almost left the vehicle without paying before she slammed the door hard and crossed the road, floating weightless to-ward the entrance.

She entered the now abandoned lobby for the second time that day, with only a man in a black tuxedo and bow tie standing at a podium beside the elevator to greet her. He po-litely asked her name then crossed it off the list before au-thorising her to proceed. Inside the elevator she pressed the button for the rooftop on the thirty-third floor. The elevator lifted and she inhaled deeply and tried to push Frederich out of her mind. She had no choice. The party was too important. How she handled this moment could impact the rest of her life. She started by checking her reflection in the mirror, paying close attention to her black dress. The sleek design accentuated her body, and the v-neck revealed the top of her breasts covered in black lace that ran over her shoulders and down her arms. It would not have been Ida's first choice. Claire, the lady at the shop, had insisted that it was the dress for her, and that she would feel more comfortable in it by the minute. Ida had no idea how much the dress was worth, but she knew it was a lot, judging by the store's location on Avenue Montaigne. Making her more nervous still was having to return the outfit the following day undamaged. If only she could have worn the dress she had brought from Berlin.

The elevator door opened and in came the sound of chatter and music. Ida turned around and put on her best smile, walking directly into the open-air party. The group closest to her stopped their conversation and began looking her up and down before smiling and resuming their conversation while taking sips of their champagne. Ida continued moving through the crowd, getting stares from almost everyone. Immediately she felt out of place. Everybody was stunningly dressed. The men had their hair trimmed and styled, and their tuxedos were a perfect fit. The attractiveness level of the women was off the scale. Many of them were almost certainly models; gorgeous with flawless, glowing skin, long legs and impeccable posture. Most faces which looked critically at Ida were either beautiful or had been made beautiful by a surgeon. Their expressions asked the question loud and clear: 'Who is this strange girl, and what is she doing here?'

Tiny Christmas lights hung above in a criss-cross fashion. There were randomly spread cocktail tables draped in white sheets, and at the far end was a band playing classical music on a small stage beside the bar. A waiter approached and offered Ida champagne, which she accepted. Standing in the middle, she realised, made her a target for attention. Everywhere she looked, eyes were pointed her way. Her body was preparing to scramble to a less exposed location but she held herself firm, even though her fingers were jittering from nervousness.

"Ida!" came a voice from the side.

Tina emerged from the crowd holding a champagne glass while walking confidently toward Ida. She had on a sparkling grey dress which continued up over her chest and wrapped around her shoulders, revealing the side of her breasts. Splits ran along both sides and made visible her fit body. As always she was wearing stilettos, which added to her already impressive height and gave her a majestic walk. With her long diamond earrings and pink lipstick she could have been straight from a movie.

"Ida, nice to see you," said Tina, smiling and reaching forward to hug her with one arm.

"You look amazing," said Ida, blinking multiple times and looking Tina up and down.

"Me?" said Tina, shaking her head. "Look at you!" she added, her face lighting up. "I knew Claire could do it. You look unbelievable!"

A smile found its way to Ida's face.

"Thanks," she said.

Tina paid close attention to Ida's mouth with a concerned look.

"What?" said Ida, raising her hand to her face.

"Oh, you've got a bit of extra lipstick there," said Tina, taking Ida by the hand and leading her to the side.

124

Tina leaned forward and inspected Ida's mouth before rubbing the side of Ida's lip with her knuckle.

"There, that's better," she said, smiling and nodding with satisfaction.

"Oh, that was silly of me. I didn't check it before I left," said Ida, remembering the moment she had been distracted by the news story.

"Don't worry. Come, I'll introduce you to some people."

Tina took Ida's hand and led her through the party crowd, drawing stares like magnets passing through shards of metal.

"Ladies, meet Ida," said Tina upon approaching two young women standing side by side, both holding their champagne glasses.

"Hi, Ida," said one young woman without any expression while waving her hand across her body. She had dark make-up, long, shiny straight blonde hair that ran down her back and a tall, skinny body.

"Hello, Ida," said the other woman with a smile, a brunette version of the first woman.

"This is Sophie," said Tina, pointing to the blonde woman who now had her attention somewhere else. "And this is Claudia," she said, pointing to the brunette. "They're both represented by an agency here in Paris."

"Nice to meet you," said Ida, unsurprised that they were models.

"Remember this face," said Tina, signalling toward Ida. "She might be designing your outfits in the future."

"Really?" said Claudia with her French accent. "That is so wonderful. We need more young designers, especially women."

"Ida brings something new to the table. She designs specifically for the empowered woman."

"Wonderful! Then she is with good company," said Claudia, signalling toward Tina.

"That's right," said Tina, grabbing Ida's hand and dragging her away. "We'll be right back, ladies."

As the two of them walked along, still drawing ample attention, Tina leaned in close to Ida.

"You see all these wandering eyes?" said Tina. "Most women have no idea what to do with this kind of power. Having every man wanting to fuck you, and every woman wanting to secretly destroy you can make life complicated. If you're not careful, it can end your career before it begins. But if you learn how to use it to your advantage, you can go as far as you want."

Ida gave Tina a tight smile and gulped.

"What did you think of Claudia and Sophie?" asked Tina.

"They seemed nice, and they're beautiful," said Ida.

"They hated you," said Tina sharply. "Both of them."

Ida flinched and turned toward Tina with a look of disbelief.

"You're a threat to them," said Tina. "Well, not yet. But you could be. And because you've stolen my attention, they hate you more."

"I didn't mean to—"

"It's not your fault, don't worry," said Tina. "It's nothing you can control. You have to get used to it. Even the men who want to sleep with you hate you. They only hide it until they get what they want. And if they don't get what they want, you can bet your life they'll show it to you then."

"Is that how it is here?" said Ida.

"Of course," said Tina. "But like I told you, you learn to relish it."

They approached the bar and Tina took Ida's half-full glass from her and laid it down.

"Two sidecars," said Tina to the bartender before turning to Ida. "Let's stay here for a while."

"Ok," said Ida.

Minutes later they had their cocktails in hand, complete with a slice of orange wedged along the tip. They stood in front of the bar taking sips and inspecting the scene around them.

"Look, there," said Tina, pointing toward a young man in a tuxedo standing among a group of four beautiful women. "Handsome, isn't he?"

He was looking directly at Ida, making no attempt to conceal it. He had light brown hair combed upwards and slightly to the side and a stubbly beard which accentuated his jawline. Through a squint his light blue eyes shone through. Without warning he broke away from his female companions and walked in Ida and Tina's direction.

"Get ready," whispered Tina.

Oh, no. Don't come here. Ida got butterflies in her belly, and tried to contain her nerves as he came near.

"You look stunning this evening," he said on approach, his full attention on Ida.

The eye contact was too much, and Ida looked away briefly before looking back and smiling.

"Terence," he said, reaching out his hand.

Ida was about to reciprocate and tell him her name, before remembering what Tina had told her earlier.

"What can I do for you, Terence?" she found herself saying.

Terence raised his eyebrows high, his hand still reached out. Ida ignored it and reached forward and rubbed on his jacket collar.

"Nice tuxedo," she said.

Terence gave Tina a bewildered looked, to which she offered no help, only shrugging and smiling.

"Thanks," he said. "So I don't get a name?"

"Not yet," said Ida, now feeling much more confident maintaining deep eye contact, knowing Tina was standing beside her.

A smile betrayed Terence and he shook his head while biting his lip.

"I won't bullshit you," he said. "Now I'm twice as intrigued."

"I'm glad you're not going to bullshit me," said Ida. "If you do, then you'll never get that name. Or anything else."

"Fair enough," he said, narrowing his gaze and turning serious, even appearing vulnerable for a split second. "I'm going to return to my friends. I have no doubt we'll run into each other again tonight."

"If it's meant to be, then sure," said Ida.

He nodded, almost chuckling.

"See you soon," he said.

"I look forward to it," said Ida.

Terence turned around and rejoined his group, who enthusiastically welcomed him back while glancing curiously in Ida and Tina's direction.

Tina said nothing, only squeezed her nose up and stared expectantly at Ida.

"He was cute," said Ida, her face remaining stone cold.

Tina snickered and shook her head in disbelief.

"Well done," she said with an earnest expression. "Well done."

"Thank you," said Ida, a sly smirk on her face, having enjoyed the rush of the encounter.

"Let's go for another wander, shall we?" said Tina. "See how many more hearts you can break."

"Sounds fun," said Ida with a nod, once again following Tina's lead.

The place was crawling, with people laughing in fits, yelling over each other, migrating around the room with beers pressed close to their bodies. At one point there was a collective scream, with a group scrambling in various directions as a cup full of beer flew into the air. Deciphering what was happening inside the Stern and Dolly was going to be tough, figured Frederich, especially from across the road while sitting in his car.

It was a chilly evening, and the street remained as quiet as a suburban street should in the middle of the week. The cold had seeped into the cabin of the car over the passing hours and was working its way through Frederich's feet and fingers. It did little to distract him. He understood the scope of the challenge which awaited him.

Bibby, Dikka, Pistol, Faust and Vent; all five were at the Stern and Dolly for the second straight night with no apparent hit jobs to keep them busy. Bibby was by far the loudest and most animated, commanding attention with his sheer size. Faust the boxer stood close to a young woman in a tight white singlet, the two of them talking intimately into each other's ears. The more they drank, the more enthusiastically the woman laughed and laid hands on Faust. At one point they disappeared into the crowd and did not appear again. At 10:41 pm Vent came outside to take a phone call, standing away from the pub by the side of the road before going back inside. The call did not seem urgent. Frederich waited and watched, keenly aware of the deadline. The longer Vent and his friends remained in there, the more the risk increased. To Frederich's relief, he got a break at 12:13 am. Dikka, Pistol, Faust and Vent came bursting through the door, swaying here and there, obviously under the influence of Liam the bartender's booze. Bibby was missing, and it was almost four hours until deadline. Frederich thought for a moment, then decided to follow them by foot. He would discreetly deal with these guys then get back to Bibby. In any case, better four out of five than none, he figured.

He exited the car and locked it then crossed the road, passing the Stern and Dolly and following the four men while maintaining a safe distance. They led him to the end of the street then turned right, followed the road for a while then went left. *Pistol's street*. As Frederich had predicted, Pistol hugged and bumped fists with each of his friends then stumbled onto his yard, heading toward his front door while the rest continued down the path. Frederich rushed forward. He neared Pistol's front yard and crept over the grass with his breath held. The hunting knife was already in his hand. Pistol was at the front door with his hand in his pocket, digging for his keys while brushing his hair back. Frederich sped up once he left the grass, scurrying over the concrete. Pistol had barely begun turning around when Frederich snatched a handful of his hair and pulled his head back with one hard jolt, before slicing his neck open with the hunting knife. Pistol's reflexes were as slow as Frederich had imagined them to be, having smelt the stench of beer on him from metres away. Frederich remained standing there as Pistol tumbled to the ground, with only the sound of him gasping and groaning for his life in the darkness. Pistol's struggle for survival gradually died down until the night-time silence returned.

Frederich took off immediately, holding the bloody knife backwards and tucking it along his forearm as he sprinted again over the yard and back in the direction of the remaining three men. At the end of Pistol's street was a T-intersection. *Left or right?* He relied on his ears, hearing the faint sound of a man raising his voice to the right. The bending road kept the men out of sight until Frederich came around and caught a glimpse of them turning into an open space between two houses. He accelerated to catch up, appearing at the corner where the men had previously been and finding them crossing through a park. It was high risk, but if he pulled it off he would avoid the chance of things getting complicated later if they split up. He took a couple of deep calming breaths and pulled the stun gun out of his inside jacket pocket and moved forward. Dikka trailed the group and was the first to hear Frederich approach.

"What the fuck?" he blurted as he saw Frederich approach, his shaved head pulling backwards in surprise and his huge eyes lighting up in the night.

Dikka's hearing was sharp, but his reflexes were terrible. Alcohol again proved a deciding factor. Before Dikka could react, Frederich punched the stun gun into his hip, and within seconds had forced him to ground. Vent's reflexes worked quicker than his friend's, and almost immediately he sprinted away. Frederich dropped the stun gun and flipped the hunting knife around so it was straight in his hand. He reached back and flung it forward, hitting Vent between the shoulder blades. Vent grunted loudly and fell to the ground, the knife wedged in his back. Meanwhile, Faust came forward in a boxing stance and sent a right hook at Frederich's head. Frederich dodged it and scrambled to the side to create space. Faust came at him again with two jabs, which Frederich fended off with his arms raised to protect his face. When the right hook returned he ducked it while knowing the fight was already over. It seemed Faust had assumed they were sticking to boxing rules. Frederich had no code of honour guiding him. He only cared about his deadline. With Faust off-balance, Frederich rose up and kneed him in the balls, then hit him with a mighty hook.

There was no time to survey the fallout or think. *Terminate and conceal.* Frederich went over to Vent, who was grunting and scrambling across the grass on his stomach in obvious pain. He took the knife out of Vent's back and slit his throat. Dikka was laying on his side, still crippled by the stun gun, before Frederich also slit his throat. Faust was on his knees, struggling to get back up. Frederich picked up the stun gun and gave him a second jolt for good measure before dealing him the same fate as Dikka and Vent.

A bright light approached when a car passed by along the street, oblivious to the slaughter taking place in the shadows. Darkness was Frederich's ally as he dragged each of the bodies behind the bushes by the fence, confident they would remain hidden until morning. He wiped the blade of his knife clean on the grass then packed it inside his jacket along with his stun gun before making back for the Stern and Dolly.

"What the hell was taking them so long?" thought Vidrik as he pushed the stairway door open and went up to the rooftop. Radara was toying with him, he decided, taking her sweet time and enjoying herself while he festered and waited.

He climbed the final step then stopped just behind the door, carefully pulling down on the handle and pushing it open a crack. A pair of large pot plants concealed the entrance to the stairs and blocked Vidrik's line of sight. He slowly worked the door open and emerged onto the terrace and crept to a position behind the bushes. He shook his head disapprovingly as he studied the buffoons in tuxedos trying to impress a bunch of hussies with short skirts and fake tits.

"Where are you, my little princess?" he whispered to himself, carefully inspecting each woman.

No sign of them. He paused before slowly emerging from behind the plants to widen his angle of view. A sudden jolt shot through him. He focussed his eyes and took her in, feeling ripples of pleasure below his belly button. Her dress stopped just above her knees, and her ass looked marvellous and supple as she stretched the material with her movements. He zoned out for a moment looking at her chest then continued upwards to her face. She looked poised, laughing and confidently waving her arm around as she spoke, capturing the attention of everyone listening to her. Radara was having quite the influence on her, it seemed. Or was it the alcohol?

First Vidrik thought it was just him, but when he rechecked the surroundings he saw at least a dozen eyes pointed in Ida's direction. He was not at all surprised; he had known her potential from the beginning. He felt incredibly alive and light on his feet, his skin tingling all over. The colours around him grew bright and vibrant. The sound of chatter and music rushed in and filled his ears as though he were hearing it for the first time, while the influx of energy pulsing through his body threatened to overwhelm him. What was going on? Then he made the connection. He took hold of his smartphone and snapped a photo of her — for later. Her posture, her smile, the way she was glowing. It was pure perfection.

"There you are, my queen," he whispered to himself.

"Lace is like icing on a cake. You need to use *just* the right amount," said Ida, squinting one eye and signalling a tiny amount with her thumb and index finger.

"Are you sure you're talking about icing?" said another woman, mimicking Ida's hand expression and causing the entire group to break out into laughter.

"I agree," said Claudia with a thoughtful nod when the fever died down. "I have always felt this."

"My mother used to wear too much of it," said Ida, shaking her head disapprovingly.

"Tina, I want Ida to design me something," declared Claudia. "Please connect her with my agent."

"Of course," said Tina, smiling politely and stepping forward after having had her attention somewhere else. "Oh, Ida, darling, you have something on your cheek."

"Do I?" said Ida. "One moment."

She pulled her handbag forward and began digging inside for her makeup mirror. Her motor skills felt off from one too many cocktails. Maybe it was best to slow down. *Why though?* She was having such a good time.

Her hands latched onto a round object inside her handbag, and she pulled out her pocket mirror and snapped it open, raising it to her face to see what Tina meant. There was a tiny, barely noticeable black speck on her face. She cleaned it off with her fingertip, wondering why Tina would even bother pointing it out. Maybe Tina had meant something else. She moved the mirror to the other side of her face but saw nothing. Her attention shifted temporarily to the background, and she felt her gaze drawn to the plants beside the elevator. There was someone there, standing by himself and staring in her direction. He was wearing a black turtleneck. Her arm flinched hard when she finally recognised him, and she gasped as a violent pain exploded in her chest.

15

While Ida had her attention on her pocket mirror, the rest of the group's focus had shifted away. Only Tina remained watching her with a curious expression.

"Got it?" asked Tina.

"What?" said Ida, looking up from the mirror and shaking her head.

Tina leaned over and inspected Ida's cheek.

"Yes, it's gone," she said with a tight-lipped smile. "Another drink?"

How the hell did he find me?

"Ida?"

"Yes," said Ida. "Let's get another drink."

"Ok," said Tina, already walking in the direction of the bar. "The girls had to go to the bathroom. They said they'd join us later."

"Ok," said Ida.

"Are you ok?" asked Tina. "Have you had too much to drink?"

"No, I'm fine," said Ida.

Keep it together.

"You sure?"

"Yes," said Ida. "I need to go to the bathroom quickly. I'll meet you at the bar."

"Ok, hurry back. My friend just texted me. He'll be here any minute."

"Ok, great. I'll be right back."

Ida walked to the bathroom while trying to not appear in a rush, doing her best to avoid looking in the direction of the plants. Inside she ignored Claudia and Sophie standing at the sink and went straight into the cubicle, where she broke out into a sweat and began shivering. What was she going to do? Should she tell Tina about Vidrik? Should she call the police? Should she try to escape? Could Tina even help her? Probably not. They were on a rooftop, thirty-three levels above ground. He would easily hunt her down. The police would be no use against him. *Or would they?* She felt helpless, unable to think straight, unable to escape the feeling that Vidrik was going to find her and kill her.

The shivering would not stop. Ida wanted to scream out loud or kick something. *Oh, God. Think!* What else could she do? She dug into her handbag and found her wallet, searched between her receipts and business cards until she found the paper that Frederich had given her. She could scarcely believe what she was about to do. There was no other choice. She reached into her handbag again and took out her phone, ready to dial the organisation which months earlier had tried to kill her.

The adrenaline had caught up with Frederich once he made it back to the Stern and Dolly. The driver's seat felt claustrophobic now. He was acutely aware of the sound of his breath, could feel every micro-droplet of sweat covering his body. He knocked his fingertips continuously on the dashboard, unable to hold back the raw energy inside him.

The seconds seemed to pass slower for him than they did for the outside world. He resorted to deep breathing and tapping his foot while intently watching the inside of the pub, ready to pounce on the tiniest movement Bibby made.

The last surviving group member was perched on a stool, leaning back on the bar with an arrogant grin, unaware of the fate of his friends. It was 1:43 am, and the crowd inside the Stern and Dolly had barely thinned out. How were they still open, wondered Frederich? The door of the place had listed the closing time as 11:30 pm. It was evident from Bibby's body language that he had something to do with the lack of curfew. The patrons inside the pub seemed to orbit around him. Frederich had to think back on his fight with Scheffler, how difficult it had been to battle against such raw strength. He was hoping that intoxication would again prove a helpful handicap.

He shook when his phone vibrated in his pocket and kept his eyes on Bibby while he answered.

"Abel," said Gerricks. "Listen, there isn't much time. Your girlfriend called. Ida."

"Ida?" said Frederich, sitting up in his seat.

"Yeah. She's in trouble, said Vidrik is after her."

Frederich's grip around the phone tightened. *Vidrik.*

"Where is she?" he said.

"In Paris. I'm going to send you a web address where you can follow her coordinates. I've got her GPS connected to our server."

"Ok. I'm still in London. Can you send someone in the meant—"

"No fucking way," Gerricks interjected. "You know we can't do that. Everyone's tied up. I shouldn't even be wasting time telling you this."

"Shit," whispered Frederich.

"Gotta go. Good luck."

The call ended abruptly.

Frederich stopped breathing. A suffocating pressure clamped down on his temples like a vice, grinding against his skull, pushing him deeper into the abyss where the fires of hell had blown wide open. He burst out of the car, leaving the door open, and stomped across the road. The front door of the Stern and Dolly was held open by a pair of men preparing to go home, and Frederich forced his way past them.

Bibby was still on his stool, but the grin had left his face. He lifted his head, staring directly at Frederich, who had reached into his pocket and drawn his pistol. Screams broke out, and people scrambled in every direction. As Frederich prepared to pull the trigger, a mysterious hand pushed his arm up from the side, causing the bullet to fire into the air. Frederich began tussling with the invader, while Bibby sprang up and ran in his direction before roundhouse kicking him in the stomach with such force that his guts exploded with pain and he went crashing through the front window before his head smacked into the concrete, leaving him temporarily disoriented. He rolled to his side over the broken glass and groaned, trying to focus on the enormous figure emerging from inside. Bibby was thick all over, with large chunks of muscle creating an armour over his entire body. He had a wrinkled forehead, a long angled nose and uneven eyes accompanied by thick, slanted eyebrows. He grunted and stepped forward, now holding a crowbar. Frederich struggled up onto his feet, lightheaded but oozing with adrenaline.

Bibby approached and Frederich shuffled to the side, dodging the crowbar which came toward his head. Bibby swung over and again, grunting each time. Meanwhile, the crowd had emerged from inside, emboldened by Bibby's offensive, and they encircled the pair as they stood locked in battle. The smartphones came out immediately, with at least a dozen cameras suddenly pointed in Frederich's direction. One of them flashed in Frederich's face as someone took a picture, momentarily blinding him, followed by another swing of Bibby's crowbar. Frederich felt the metal brush against the top of his head as he scurried to dodge it, falling to the ground in the process. Bibby tried to stomp on his hip while he was down, forcing him to roll to the side. He scrambled back to his feet, panting loudly, his attention scattered by the chaos around him. The shouting grew hysterical, as each person vied for an unobstructed view of the fight. An attack could now come from any direction if someone was feeling bold enough. *Focus,* came Kraas' voice, just like it always had when Frederich's senses got the better of him during an especially challenging training sequence. He clenched his fists tight enough for them to ache then pushed his feet into the ground and bent his knees, breathing deeply into his core. Bibby snickered and approached, while a woman pushed her smartphone out to film closer to the action. Frederich snatched it from her and tossed it at Bibby, hitting him in the forehead.

"Hey!" yelled the woman.

Bibby scowled and raised his hand to touch the place of impact.

"You dirty bastard!" he yelled, a mark appearing where the phone had hit him.

"Get him, Bibby!" said the woman whose phone now lay smashed on the ground.

"Teach that flog a lesson!" someone else yelled out from the crowd.

Frederich narrowed his focus further, filtering out everything but the monster in front of him. Once he weaved out of the way of another crowbar attack, he went on the offensive, landing punch after punch into Bibby's body then jabbing him in the nose and landing a stiff hook into his chin. He went deeper inside himself, channelling his rage into each attack, landing them with more and more ease as he lost himself in a furious flow. Bibby was unable to keep up, and his attempts to block Frederich's attacks fell further out of sync as Frederich exposed every vulnerable area he could find. A point came when Bibby stopped resisting, swaying to the side, straightening up again, then finally collapsing to the ground, his face bloodied. By now Frederich was too far gone, leaping onto Bibby and piling a flurry of punches into the barely conscious man's face. He momentarily lost touch with his body as *it* came, before he blacked out.

When he came back he had multiple hands holding him tightly in place. He looked around and noticed that he was in the grip of four men, while Bibby lay motionless on the ground. Frederich's rapid breathing gradually seeped back into consciousness, his shoulders dropped, and his body returned to him. The crowd was silent now, all eyes were on him, with half a dozen smartphones still trained in his direction.

"Is he alright?" said someone, as a man crouched down to check on Bibby.

Bibby groaned on cue.

"Yeah, he's alright," said the man.

A young guy with blonde spikes, grey jeans and a white t-shirt lowered his phone, grinning widely with his eyes ablaze.

"Holy shit, that was awesome!" he yelled out.

Frederich's captors loosened their grip, leaving him free to stand on his own. Frederich looked around, studying the incredulous, slack-jawed faces of the crowd.

"Who is this guy? Anyone seen him before?"

"Nah, never seen him."

"What's your name?" asked the excited young man with the blonde spikes.

"Shit, Liam's calling the cops," said a voice in the crowd.

Frederich shook himself out of his daze and broke away. He picked up his pistol from the ground then staggered across the road and returned to his car, remembering what had caused him to snap in the first place. He switched on the engine and drove off. When the adrenaline subsided further his knuckles began throbbing with pain. *Dammit.* Bibby was still alive, he realised. That was out of his control now. The killing window was gone. The priority was Ida. He took his phone out and dialled her number but got no answer. He tried again with the same result. Then he tapped into his messages and opened the web address Gerricks had sent him. The map of Paris appeared, along with a blue dot on the west side. He closed the screen then dialled Gerricks.

"Yeah," said Gerricks, after the phone rang for a long time.

"I need to get to Paris right away," said Frederich.

There was a short pause.

"We've got a plane at London City Airport. I'll tell them you're coming."

16

The tip of Ida's finger rubbed against the edge of the cocktail glass in a circular motion while she ruminated about the danger she was in. The League Of Reckoning had not been as helpful as she had hoped. The man who answered her call said he would 'see what he could do.' 'No promises,' he had declared before hanging up. For now, Ida had to assume she was alone. A throbbing pressure drummed in her ears, and her legs felt weak. What was Vidrik doing in Paris, and how had he found her?

Tina had her arms crossed and was facing away while a severely drunken Claudia chewed her ear off. She sighed and abruptly excused herself with a raised palm and approached Ida.

"Time to go," she said curtly. "He's here. He's waiting for us downstairs."

Ida's finger froze on the edge of the cocktail glass. The floor beneath her fell. *Oh, no.* How could she have missed it? There was no time to ask why; she only knew that if she went downstairs with Tina, she would be dead. She looked around frantically without moving her head, and spotted Terence standing in the distance alone with one hand in his pocket and the other holding a lit cigarette. She walked away from Tina without saying anything and placed her glass on the bar before approaching Terence, who looked up as she came near.

"I think it's time to go home," she said.

Terence held her gaze for several seconds then tossed the cigarette away. He rotated his body and held his elbow out, and Ida clasped onto it. Together they made for the elevator, during which Ida turned in Tina's direction. What she saw almost made her jump. Tina's entire face had changed to the point that Ida could not recognise it. Terence pressed the elevator button while Ida remained gripped by Tina's fiery stare. The door opened, and Ida and Terence got in. Tina stood in place, her glare so penetrating and hateful looking that it choked the air out of Ida. The door then closed shut, finally allowing Ida to release herself from Tina's grasp, and she was able to breathe again.

"What the hell was he thinking!" yelled Scheffler, slamming his fist on the desk.

"No idea," said Gerricks, cowering slightly and leaning away before straightening again. "But it's going viral over social media. A hundred million views and counting. The way he tore that Bibby guy up got people talking. I don't blame them. Look at how quick he's moving, how crisp his punches are. I've never seen anything like it."

"You done?" said Scheffler, giving Gerricks a hard stare.

"It's not a good look for us," said Gerricks, lowering his head.

"No, it's not," said Scheffler while massaging his temple.

Scheffler was already on edge after Barcelona. Now this. *Damn it, Abel.*

"We'll have to deal with it later," he said. "What's happening on the radar?"

"Our lieutenants sent word that they're ready and in place," said Gerricks.

Scheffler peeped at the clock. 2:57 am. He began pacing from side to side while watching the surveillance screens, which were flicking between suburban houses, mansions, apartment blocks, hotels and warehouses. Most locations remained eerily motionless. 2:58 am. He stopped pacing and started bouncing on his toes, then ran his hand through his hair. *I should be out there.* 2:59 am. The first soldiers appeared on the screen, creeping forward from their positions, dressed in black and armed with rifles. Scheffler clenched his jaw.

Piotr gripped the knuckle duster tightly. Ralph's battering ram weighed more than fifteen kilos, and Ralph was a natural brute, so it was in the right hands. Ralph turned to Piotr and they exchanged nods in the dark, before Ralph swung his arms back and smashed into the door just below the lock. The porch quaked beneath Piotr's feet while sections of the door cracked open. Ralph immediately swung the red tube of steel back again and this time managed to smash the door open.

The battering ram fell to the ground and Ralph pulled out his pistol. He stood out of the way and nudged the destroyed door open then waited for Piotr to enter first. Piotr took off, turning into a dark hallway. The bedroom was the first door on the left. He went straight in and found an empty bed illuminated by moonlight with the sheets pulled to the side, revealing the crease of the body that had been sleeping there. He turned around quickly and saw Ralph looking at him from the doorway with his pistol pointed down the hall. Piotr shook his head, and Ralph took that as a cue to continue forward. The bathroom across was empty. Piotr checked the kitchen with the same result. Ralph came out of the living room without finding anything. Piotr then pulled the door open for the crammed storage room and shut it again. *Where are you, you slippery bastard?* After a short pause his feet led him back to the bedroom. He listened carefully in the silence until it occurred to him there was one place he had not yet looked. *Got you!* he thought, ducking below the bed.

There was nothing, only a build-up of dust.

A gun went off outside and Piotr rose up with a violent jerk. He plucked his knuckle dusters off his hands and tossed them onto the bed then fumbled with his pistol as he took it out of his pocket. Two more bullets fired outside. He bolted out of the room and into the hallway. His heart was thumping like a drum. Moonlight was now coming through the laundry door, and a breeze blew inside. Outside had fallen eerily silent. It was too dangerous to go out that way, he figured. He turned back for the front door and carefully stuck his head outside, looking both ways. With agonisingly slow movements he stepped out onto the porch and went right in the direction of the gunshots, ducking below the windows as he passed them. At the corner of the house he stopped again and listened. The sheer adrenaline made him suddenly dizzy, and he had trouble focussing his eyes. The thought of going out there caused his hands to begin shaking uncontrollably. He pushed his back against the wall and tried to take a calming breath with no effect. The shaking spread to his entire body and his teeth began chattering. He worried that if he stayed there any longer, he would pass out. He remained frozen, paralysed by fear. Only the even greater fear of death forced him to act.

"Shit, shit, shit," he whispered.

He sprinted out from his position and into the open. The gunshot that immediately came from the back fence was terrifyingly loud but he continued forward, propelled by pure instinct. The man was crouched in the corner between the shed and the fence, shrouded in moonlight and pointing his gun forward. Piotr went out of his mind and fired a flurry of bullets. The man seemed to jerk, and Piotr fired one final shot as he came near. The man slumped over to his side. Piotr slowed to a halt and lowered his gun, gasping for air, barely able to feel his body. The man remained motionless on his side, wearing only shorts. It occurred to Piotr then that he had been running at an angle the whole time, which had probably saved his life. He also had no idea which of his bullets had struck the man, or how many shots the man had fired during that time.

He remained at a distance, not daring to move any closer, terrified of seeing the man's lifeless stare judging him from the beyond. He turned away to the side instead, and found Ralph's body on the grass, his neck and chest covered in blood.

"It's escalating," said Gerricks, his head cocked to the side. "Look. Here and here."

Scheffler leaned forward and paid close attention to the screens. A soldier with a body camera had just burst into a warehouse when at least a dozen armed men swarmed him with rifles. The camera shook, and the soldier fell to the ground while the armed men continued past him. Another two soldiers were escorting someone out of a building before the footage turned chaotic, the camera spinning in all directions. A crowd of people in a public square in Stockholm ran away screaming as a gunfight broke out. Another screen showed only smoke.

"Doesn't look good," said Gerricks.

Scheffler looked into space while rubbing his chin. Most of the targets were supposed to be shocked from their slumber and taken in with minimal fuss. Instead, mayhem had broken out almost from the get-go.

"How many casualties?" said Scheffler.

"Hard to tell. There's too much going on. Fifty? Hundred? It's climbing."

Scheffler tapped his fingers on the desk while grinding his teeth. If he was going to call in reinforcements, now was the time. There would be no victory without them, and Scheffler wanted to triumph more than anything. Everything he did for The League was in service of that goal. There was just one problem: if he did call in the reinforcements, all-out war would break out on the streets. The fall-out would be horrific. Civilians would surely enter the crossfire. Unforeseen consequences would ripple for days and weeks, possibly longer. It was a nightmare in the making. The greatest weakness of their plan was that they had no idea of the strength of their enemy.

Scheffler was forced to think back to his first mission in Kosovo, the one that 'never happened,' where hostilities between the Kosovo Liberation Army and the Yugoslavians were raging, and an undercover MI5 agent remained trapped in the Drenica Valley. The untested Scheffler was a last-minute addition to the unit of five men tasked with extracting the MI5 agent in a nighttime operation. Scheffler could still vividly see the faces of his fellow soldiers in the dark, glistening with sweat and adrenaline in their eyes after they had been forced into the forest by unexpected heavy bombing. Their mission was off the books, so they had no way of calling in help, and both the KLA and Yugoslavian Army were potential 'enemies.' The plan had been to move along a deserted road, sneak into the village, get the agent and be out by sunrise. Three days later they were deep in the woods with foreign soldiers crawling the area. Something serious and unexpected had happened, and their location had become a point of sudden interest for both sides. An argument broke out between the members of Scheffler's unit. They looked to their squad leader Jack for a way out. Jack insisted that saving the agent was a lost cause. He established a new landing zone ten kilometres south and prepared his men to move out. Scheffler was livid. How could they give up? There *had* to be a way to complete the mission. He told Jack he had a plan to get the agent out by himself, and if he was not back in five hours they could leave without him. Jack outright refused, so Scheffler waited until Jack was distracted and took off anyway without his squad leader's permission.

The village was two kilometres away, and KLA soldiers remained scattered in every direction. Using darkness as cover, Scheffler lay charges in three separate locations and set them to detonate ten minutes apart. The first explosion went off, and as predicted, the KLA soldiers moved in that direction. He shifted to the edge of the village, and the next charge went off. He crept along the streets while following his map. As he found the house where the agent was meant to be waiting, the third charge went off. KLA soldiers sprinted past before he worked his way around the house. The door for the underground bunker was in the backyard beneath the shed. Scheffler pulled it open and went down into the tiny space, ignoring the stench, where he found the man he was tasked with saving with a bullet hole in the head.

There was no time for emotion. Scheffler took the treacherous path back to the forest, where to his surprise his unit was still waiting for him. He handed the agent's belongings to Jack, including a small diary and a wallet with a picture of what looked like the man's daughter. They made it to the LZ and were extracted without incident.

The mission was a failure, but at least the agent's family would have closure. They could mourn without the torture of false hope, without a lifetime of 'what ifs.' After the mission, Scheffer was reprimanded for refusing the orders of a superior, then promoted for his bravery. Jack had been instrumental in him getting a pass. Scheffler had put his life on the line, refusing to concede defeat. He had somehow found a way.

This time was different. It was not his life that would be at risk.

He knew what he had to do, but the thought of going through with it made his stomach turn. He desperately sought out a magical solution but came up short. Facts were facts. It was turning into a bloodbath, and the longer it went on, the more men they were going to lose. He clenched his fist until it began to tremble, until the nails cut into his palm. He scanned every screen desperately for signs of victory, anything that might signal the winds were about to change. All he saw was one of his soldiers running for his life before a splatter of blood caused by a headshot sent him spilling to the ground.

Scheffler eased his fisted grip. He had seen enough.

"Tell everyone to pull back," he said.

Gerricks turned from his screen and gave Scheffler a bewildered stare.

"Serious?"

Scheffler rubbed his temples. *I can't believe I'm doing this.*

"Yes. Full retreat," he said with a low, thick voice.

"You got it," said Gerricks.

Scheffler stood up and left the room, then went into his office and shut the door. He slumped into his chair and frowned, disgusted with himself. There was a painful lump in his throat. He covered his face with his hands, unable to bear it all. There would be no victory, he realised, no glory to be had. Until his death, he would never forget that his first significant operation as General was an absolute and total failure, and there was nothing he could do about it.

17

The streets were deserted. Even in heels, Ida marched quickly down the sidewalk while Terence struggled to keep up with her.

"Hey, slow down!" he said with a chuckle.

Ida checked behind them for any sign of Vidrik then crossed the road and went in the direction of the square which she had passed through earlier.

"Hey, stop for a second!" said Terence, placing a hand on Ida's waist from behind.

Ida stopped and huffed impatiently.

"What's the hurry?" said Terence, searching Ida's face.

"We can't stay here," said Ida. "I'll explain once we're safe."

"Safe?" said Terence, cocking his head back. "From what?"

"I don't have time to explain," said Ida and took off again.

"Why do I always go for the crazy ones?" came Terence's voice from a distance.

Ida approached another deserted street. *Where is everyone?* Her ears prickled. She listened in the distance to what sounded like rattling, accompanied by a sudden and strong booming noise. The rattling continued, only abating for split seconds at a time. The sound of a siren grew louder, before a police car eventually raced by with its lights on. Terence's footsteps approached slowly from behind.

"Can you hear that?" he said. "I think that's gunfire."

Ida turned her head suddenly and gasped when she saw a shadow move in the far distance behind them. She got déjà vu while looking at Terence, remembering the guy who had tried to chat her up at Gorbachev's. The image of him splayed over the step of her building with his throat cut made Ida's heart race. She had made a severe mistake exposing Terence like that.

"You're in danger if you stay with me," she said. "You need to get out of here."

"What are you talking about?" said Terence, now visibly getting angry.

"I'm sorry," said Ida, pleading with her eyes.

Terence's charming facade slowly withered away. He scowled, then tensed his face and frowned. With a slow exhale and shake of the head, he finally got the message and marched off down the street.

Ida remained where she was, allowing Terence to create distance between them. Meanwhile, she bent down and took off her stilettos and tossed them aside, then pulled at her dress until she could rip a slit at the side to allow for better movement.

She took off in the opposite direction of Terence, now able to tread silently without her heels and with quicker steps. She followed the street then descended a set of stairs. When on lower ground she began to run, crossing a multi-lane road and passing through a park filled with tall, thick trees. Every human-made structure around her was monumental and imposing, and with Vidrik lurking out there, she felt like a helpless ant trying to navigate a tyrannical child's play world. She ran along a small street engulfed on both sides by skyscrapers, then through another park which looked identical to the last one. She glanced behind her but saw no movement, then sprinted across another major road which led into a tunnel. She looked desperately down the way for a light, begging for a lone car to drive by and save her. After a long wait, her panic grew unbearable, and her sense of dread forced her to continue forward through the concrete wilderness.

Two sets of stairs led her down to even lower ground where she stopped behind a bush and listened out for Vidrik between heavy breaths. She remained where she was for a long time, listening, anticipating, not daring to move in case she gave herself away. The stillness of the night left her feeling isolated and alone, yet she took comfort in the vacuum of silence, which was tainted only by the whooshing and rattling from events happening elsewhere in the city. Then a tapping sound penetrated her bubble, sending ripples of terror shooting through her. Footsteps. Slow, deliberate echoes from above. She bolted off, speeding through a flurry of street lights and grey walls and windows, her bare feet thumping with pain as they collided with the concrete. Her chest grew tight from the lack of oxygen, which the adrenaline forced her to ignore. The Gare de La Défense train station zipped by as she found herself on the esplanade. Her panic pulled her along, deeper into the growing nightmare, with bright signs, eerily empty restaurants and bizarre artistic sculptures contributing to the surreal ride of terror.

She turned her head mid-sprint and almost screamed when she saw him. Vidrik was now at the far back of the esplanade running straight for her. She sped up again, dashing past the enormous fountain of water and through an open stretch flanked on both sides by hedges. A series of steps appeared in her way and she leapt over them as far as her legs would take her. More obstacles appeared. Benches, bicycles, electric scooters. She navigated through them all. Her terror and desperation grew. Meanwhile, despair began to seep in. How would she keep this up? Vidrik was going to catch her, and he was going to kill her.

To her surprise, she found herself slowing down. *Stop running*, a voice told her. She listened to it and finally stopped, sucking large gulps of air deep into her belly, forcing her scattered focus back into her body. Overwhelmed and unable to expend any more of her energy on fleeing, she clenched her fists and began yelling at the top of her lungs in the form of a war cry, releasing all her pent up frustration and panic.

Vidrik's footsteps approached from behind. She turned around and saw him between the hedges sauntering toward her with his twisted smile, still panting from the chase. Her body trembled and her chest heaved up and down. Vidrik approached and slowly circled her, evaluating her with his eyes before coming closer, stopping barely a metre away. She clenched her teeth and stood upright with her fists held tight, refusing to look into his eyes.

"Naughty girl," he said, reaching out and placing the back of his hand against her sweat-covered cheek.

The touch of him electrified her. She reached up and grasped his arm, snatching it forward and turning to her side while bringing him to ground in one smooth move. He was not stunned for long, growling and leaping on top of her while forcing her down. The slap to her face came from nowhere and left her stunned. He slapped her over again in a fit while she struggled to push him off. She pulled her arms up to protect her head. He punched her in the side of her stomach instead, and she yelled out in pain.

"You dirty!" he said with a hideous shriek as he continued to strike her. "Filthy!" he yelled, hitting her once more. "Disgusting!"

The insults set her off again, and she began yelling and striking back.

"Bastard!" she yelled, slapping his arms away and pushing upward with her body.

His rage grew unhinged, and his strikes became harder and more rapid, as a war of attrition broke out between them. Ida's body screamed out in pain but she refused to give up, knowing that he had snapped, had gone beyond the point of return. Her instincts compelled her to fight, assuring her that he was going to brutally murder her if she gave up.

Two loud bangs erupted nearby in rapid succession. A third one came even closer, piercing Ida's ears. Vidrik rolled off her and lifted his head, before his eyes lit up and he scrambled away. A fourth crack followed him before he disappeared behind the hedge. Ida struggled to lift her body. She looked in the direction of where the bullets came, then gasped in disbelief.

Bent down on one knee was Frederich, his gun pointed ahead with both hands and his finger on the trigger.

Frederich got to his feet and ran forward while maintaining a tight grip on the pistol. He glanced at Ida to make sure she was ok then continued past her, slowing down as he neared the hedges and carefully ducked his head around the corner. The crack of Vidrik's bullet came almost immediately from the top of the stairs, and Frederich jumped back. He turned to Ida and signalled furiously for her to find cover, to which she scrambled to her feet and stumbled the other way, taking shelter behind the hedge on the other side. Frederich listened carefully, hearing quick footsteps which grew progressively further away. He cautiously shuffled around and caught sight of Vidrik disappearing behind a white building. His body willed him to chase, to finally give Vidrik the bullet in the head he deserved. *Kill him! Don't let him get away again.* Frederich fought with the impulse while he weighed up the situation. Vidrik had the high ground. He was a sharpshooter, and he had plenty of places to hide and get off a clean shot.

Not today, Frederich told himself. If Vidrik took him out, Ida was dead. He had to get her somewhere safe. Only then could he decide the next move. He remained scanning the area with his pistol pointed forward until his instincts were satisfied, then finally relaxed his arms and strode back to where Ida was hiding. He found her kneeling on the ground with her head bowed.

"Come," he said tenderly, placing a hand on her shoulder.

When she stood up, he took her hand and led her away, careful to put himself between her and any unexpected bullets. They zig-zagged through the esplanade and ran along the bridge above the River Seine then descended a set of stairs to the isle below, not stopping until they were safely hidden behind some trees.

18

Frederich looked at Ida properly for the first time. Her face was pale and her hair was twisted up. Her cheeks, chin and arms were scraped all over and covered in red, her nose was bleeding and a slit had opened above her eye. Frederich grimaced at the sight and bit into his jaw. *I'm going to rip that son of a bitch to shreds.* Ida said nothing, only gave him a determined stare, defiantly holding back tears. Frederich reached his hand out and gently touched her face, caressing where it had turned red. Then he reached over and hugged her, overcome with relief that she was alive. She placed her hands on his shoulders, but there was barely any life in her embrace.

"Are you ok?" he said.

Ida lowered her head and looked away from him. She sniffled.

"What are you doing here?" said Frederich. "How did he find you?"

Ida walked off abruptly and went across to the bench, which faced a small, concrete square shielded by trees. Frederich sensed he had pushed too hard. He waited where he was, leaving Ida her space. The gunfire in the distance was gone and replaced by the sound of ambulance and police sirens. The alert from Intel had gone out almost an hour ago. Full retreat. The counter-offensive was over. Frederich had no idea what had caused it, but he gathered that the operation had not gone well. He was happy to wait to find out the details. After Bibby and the scramble to get to Paris, he was sapped. He had been beside himself with worry during the flight, convinced that Ida would be dead when he got there. When he arrived, he could barely believe what he was seeing; Ida putting up the fight of her life with Vidrik viciously trying to maul her. Now there she was, her body and pride banged up, but still breathing.

"We need to get you to the hospital," he said, walking over to Ida.

She remained silent, staring off into the distance.

"Ida," said Frederich gently.

"I'm an idiot," she blurted. "Stupid!" she yelled.

"You need to tell me what happened," said Frederich.

Ida turned away and shook her head.

"Ok. You don't have to talk about it if you don't want. But we should get to the hospital and have you checked out."

"I'm fine," said Ida defiantly. "Thank you for what you did. You don't have to stay if you have somewhere else you need to be."

Frederich felt a convulsion in his stomach.

"It's not like that," he said defensively.

"No?" said Ida, turning and giving him a questioning stare. "You don't have someone else to kill tonight?"

"What's going on, Ida?"

Ida sighed and frowned. She began breathing heavily and her face turned bright red.

"Dammit!" she yelled, raising her head to the sky. "I hate this!" she screamed. "I hate Paris! I hate The League! I hate Vidrik!" She turned and looked Frederich directly in the eyes with a scorching stare, her loathing on a level he had never seen before. "I hate you!!" she screamed at him at the top of her lungs.

A searing pain cut through Frederich's chest. His eyes opened wide, his mouth fell open. The pain spread to the rest of his body while he gave Ida a confused, searching look.

"You don't mean that," he said with a croaky voice.

"Don't I?" she said, pursing her lips together and narrowing her gaze. "What happened in Poland, Frederich? One bullet wasn't enough? What kind of monster does that in front of children?"

Frederich's entire body iced over. *Monster.* He could barely fathom hearing the word coming from Ida's mouth. He lowered his head and looked away. His face grew intensely hot. It got too much. He turned his anger outwards. *How dare she!* he thought. He had saved her life twice now. What gave her the right?

"You want to talk about me?" he said with force. "What the hell are you doing here, Ida? What brought you to Paris in a fucking cocktail dress when you knew Vidrik was after you? Huh? Not enough parties for you in Berlin? There's a war happening right now. Why didn't you go home to America when you had the chance? Life too boring there? You felt you needed the rush of being hunted by a psychopath?"

"I'll do what I want!" she yelled, her scowl consuming her entire face. "I won't let Vidrik or you or anyone tell me how I should live my life!"

Frederich fell quiet.

"Shit," he mouthed, biting his lower lip.

The intensity of her rage had surprised him, not to mention his own. He had to admit the fault was not hers. Vidrik had picked her out for his own sick reasons. Her only mistake had been mingling with Elias Khartoum, and she had more than paid the price for that. Why should she let Vidrik dictate what she did? Frederich relaxed his body.

"You're right," he said. "It's not your fault. It's Vidrik's."

Ida gave Frederich a sceptical glance before her face softened somewhat, the scowl leaving her.

"But Ida, there are still consequences. You could have died tonight," he said.

Ida gave him a long blank stare while the grim idea of her death lingered in the air.

"Yeah, I know," she said wearily with a nod.

The tension had now dissipated, and silence rushed in to fill the space. Ambulance sirens continued to sound in the far distance.

"You've got some balls," said Frederich with a half-smirk. "Taking him on like that. I couldn't believe what I was seeing. A brawler in a cocktail dress, taking on a murderous maniac."

Ida snorted suddenly as a laugh broke out, her face blushing.

"I might start calling you the cocktail brawler," he added.

"Idiot," she said with a smile.

She stood up and walked toward Frederich, looking somewhat like her real self again. She reached forward and wrapped her arms around him, this time embracing him with her usual warmth.

"Thank you," she whispered into his ear.

They pulled away and locked eyes, the intensity of the moment drawing them toward each other. Frederich reached out and rubbed the area around the cut above her eye.

"Sure that doesn't hurt?" he said.

"It's ok."

He felt warm all over as his affection for Ida gushed out of him, urging him to kiss her.

"Hmm," he said, still gazing into her brown eyes. "I get why people usually kiss during moments like these."

"You want to kiss me?" asked Ida with a twinkle in her eyes.

Frederich looked deeper into her.

"No," he said, shaking his head. "Not yet."

They continued holding eye contact. The life in Ida's face showed itself to him in numerous forms which came and went like weather patterns. He witnessed sadness tinged with doubt. Her face softened and revealed her glow, which sent intense tingles through him. Then it disappeared. He looked deeper into her eyes, and narrowed his. The ferocity he witnessed had not been there before. Or had it? He had never had so much time to simply *see* her.

"You do have pretty eyes," blurted Ida.

A smile escaped him.

"Thanks," he said, struggling to push the smile down.

Ida's stare hardened and the mood turned dark again.

"Can I ask you something?" she said.

"Yes," said Frederich.

"What happened in Poland, was that what you were trying to tell me about at Lustgarten? When you said 'I'm not normal?'"

"Yeah," said Frederich, now forced to look away. "I black out when it happens."

"I couldn't believe it when I found out. It's not you."

"No, but it's a part of me."

"You can't stop it?"

"No. I see it coming, then I black out."

Ida sighed.

"What's going to happen with us, Frederich?" she said. "There's so much death everywhere."

"It's going to get worse," said Frederich. "Which is why I still think you should go home."

"Not going to happen," said Ida with a hard stare. "I'm staying right here."

"I thought you'd say that."

"I can't believe I'm saying this, but it makes sense to me now why you joined The League."

"Does it?" said Frederich.

"Yes, even though it scares the hell out of me."

"Me too," said Frederich.

"I just hope you know what you're doing. You're playing a dangerous game."

"*I'm* playing a dangerous game?" said Frederich, tilting his head.

"Yes," said Ida with a grin, pointing her finger at Frederich's chest. "You. Frederich Abel."

Frederich's pocket began vibrating. He tilted his torso and took his phone out.

"I need to take this," he said.

Ida nodded, and Frederich answered.

"Abel," said Gerricks.

"Gerricks," said Frederich, walking away from Ida.

"We've got a lock on Vidrik."

"What?" said Frederich, making a fist with his free hand. "How did you find him?"

"Our cameras have had him since he left La Défense. We want you to go after him. Can't risk letting him get away. He could lead us to Stirner. After the shitstorm last night we could use a win."

"Where is he?"

"He walked into a public park just south of where you are and we haven't seen him since. The Bois de Boulogne. I'll send you his last known location."

"Perfect," said Frederich, vitalised by the knowledge that Vidrik was still within reach.

"The city's on lockdown and crawling with cops, which means he won't have gone far. But that means you need to be double careful."

"I will," said Frederich and closed the connection.

He walked back to Ida.

"They found Vidrik?" she said.

Frederich nodded.

"You're going after him?"

Frederich nodded again.

"Go," she said. "I'll be fine."

"I know you will," said Frederich, looking deep into her eyes. "Cocktail brawler."

"Pretty eyed monster," she shot back with a weary expression.

He lingered for a moment, staring indecisively at Ida. She shook her head and pushed her eyebrows together.

"What?" she said.

"Listen," said Frederich. "If... If I don't make it back..."

"Frederich," said Ida, shuffling her weight to the other leg and appearing uncomfortable.

"No, this is important," he said. "If I don't make it back, promise me you'll be extra careful. That you won't take any more unnecessary risks."

Ida sighed loudly and bit her lip, looking away for a brief moment.

"Ok," she said with a nod. "I promise."

"Thanks," said Frederich with a soft smile.

"Your turn," said Ida. "If you do come back, promise you'll have dinner with me. One normal evening away from all this stupid death and violence."

Frederich imagined spending time with just the two of them, simply enjoying each other's company. No other place to be and no shadow hanging over them.

"I'd like that," he said.

"So come back," said Ida with longing in her gaze.

Frederich nodded, holding Ida's cheeks with his hands and resting his forehead on her's. Then he spun around and made for the stairs.

"Wait," came Ida's voice.

He stopped.

"What was that gunfire I heard before?"

He paused, then turned his head.

"War," he said.

Ida nodded, her gaze sharp and gloomy.

"Stay safe," he added before pushing his way up the stairs two steps at a time, already bracing himself for a showdown with Vidrik.

19

The time had come. Kalakia's 'Schlieffen Plan' had failed, in much the same way as its namesake.

Like the German Empire at the beginning of the 20th century, Kalakia feared that a hostile power was eclipsing him. In Germany's case it was France, Britain and the Russian Empire. The Germans believed that not making the first move would prove catastrophic in the long run. Field Marshal Alfred von Schlieffen's answer was to devise a strategy to achieve swift victory in the West against the French before concentrating the German Army's forces against Russia. This approach was meant to give the Germans the upper hand when the war inevitably escalated.

The Schlieffen Plan relied on assumptions and educated guesses. The Germans assumed the Belgians would put up little to no resistance, allowing them to pass through unhindered. They also counted on the British staying out of it, and were sure the Russians would be slow to mobilise on the Eastern Front. Much did not go to plan, and the result was the gruelling trench warfare of World War I, which spanned four terrible years.

Now Kalakia was also staring down the barrel of a drawn-out conflict. Without exception, history showed that the consolidation of power always had one of three outcomes; eventual total collapse, the splitting of the entity into one or more sub-entities, or the emergence of a stronger opposing power. Rome split in two, where the eastern Byzantine Empire endured while the western half fell apart. The Mongolian Empire collapsed. The Byzantine Empire was later swallowed whole by the Ottomans. Napoleon's France was defeated. The Ottoman Empire was eclipsed by the emerging powers in Europe.

Kalakia had long predicted the third scenario, that his grip over the globe would lead to the consolidation of an opposing power. What form it would take was anyone's guess. The League focussed its efforts solely on wiping out wealth inequality, with Kalakia refusing to pursue a global totalitarian regime. He believed that power which suffocated the freedom of the masses could never justify its authority in the long run. Tyranny was a tool to be used surgically. It did not work as a political solution. The League instead sourced its strength from its unwavering moral purpose. That was the reason Kalakia's men sacrificed their lives, and why the world never rose up in defiance. If Kalakia grew corrupt, his fraudulence would funnel down and infest the entire organisation. Allowing the nations of the world their autonomy ensured cooperation while avoiding revolt. Only one flaw remained; by transcending the world powers, Kalakia had paved the path for an upstart to establish global dominance.

The tide was changing. The balance of power could tilt at any moment, putting global stability at risk, and Kalakia had no choice but to adapt. For now, there was work to do. They had to deal with the fall-out of the mayhem from the previous night.

Kalakia had his elbow on the armrest and was rubbing his forehead as Francois dolled out reports of the damage caused, with the night-time Moscow skyline in the window as a backdrop.

"The death toll in the Americas has been the worst," said Francois. "366 soldiers dead so far. We don't have a count on the injured yet. There was resistance almost everywhere."

"It seems we have stumbled on a hornet's nest," said Kalakia.

"It doesn't look good," said Francois.

"We did find one success. We now know that Stirner has indeed recruited the underworld as the military wing of his organisation."

"But how did they know about our attack? We must have a mole. Or maybe Five Eyes sold us out?"

"Such questions are irrelevant," said Kalakia and stood up.

Francois stared at Kalakia for a moment then fell quiet, his scarred face appearing tense as he began stroking his long white goatee. Kalakia left Francois to his own wisdom and retreated inside and closed the door behind him. He went over to the large-scale world map hanging on the wall.

He moved his attention from continent to continent, taking mental note of the countless native people who lived within certain borders or across them. He considered the multi-ethnic democratic states, autocratic nations, the states currently engaged in civil wars, as well as the dizzying number of alliances which scaled the globe. He spent a long time imagining what the map would look like in a few months, or the following year, or in the years to come. Which borders would still be standing, which might be erased as demographies evolved and morphed into new alliances in an age of unprecedented connectivity. He visualised the collapse of nations and the possible emergence of continental states which coincided with the rise of a global demagogue. He remained utterly consumed, losing his sense of time, before being interrupted by Francois.

"Scheffler's here."

Kalakia nodded. Once he gathered himself he went back outside and found his General standing upright with his legs firmly planted and his arms crossed.

Kalakia passed by Scheffler and went over to the window. Scheffler's reflection appeared soon after when he stood beside Kalakia and faced in the same direction toward the skyline.

"We must discuss your decision-making process, Vincent," said Kalakia.

"Right," said Scheffler.

"I understand that you are in unfamiliar territory, being thrust into this kind of leadership position at such a vicarious time."

"I don't want to make excuses."

"No, I know you are above such things. Excuses will not benefit us, in any case. Tell me, what caused you to carry out the incursion in Barcelona? Surely you had a compelling reason."

"It looked like something big was going on in there. I thought it might be important to find out—"

"What did I say at the council of war?" interjected Kalakia.

"Yeah, you're right. I buggered up."

"Your suspicions may have been warranted. Inaction may have cost us. But you do not exist in a vacuum. You are part of an interconnected family. Every decision you make impacts thousands of lives. Global stability could collapse, simply because you could not control your impulses. Do you not understand this?"

"I do," said Scheffler. "I take full responsibility for what happened."

Kalakia nodded approvingly and studied Scheffler's face. The strain of being General was showing. Scheffler's eyes looked weary and doubtful, with dark patches beneath them. His lips were pressed tightly together and his mouth was downturned.

"Tell me why you ordered a full retreat," said Kalakia.

Scheffler cleared his throat.

"Didn't have a choice," he said. "It wasn't an easy decision, I'll tell you. We would have found ourselves in a bloodbath if we dug in. We needed to regroup."

"The casualties in Europe appear to be the lowest because of your decision. And you were correct. Fighting on would have been counter-productive, to say the least."

"So…"

"You were in a difficult place, and you made the correct decision."

"I'm glad to hear you say that," said Scheffler, exhaling slowly.

"Now, how will you deal with Frederich Abel? That reckless brawl could have cost us dearly."

"Looks like he flipped out again. Not sure how long we should tolerate it."

"You wish to terminate him?"

Scheffler went quiet for a long time.

"No," he finally said. "I want him on our team."

"You failed to tame him during his training. How do you intend to reign him in now?"

"He's on Vidrik's tail at the moment, so we've got no choice but to let him keep going. He could lead us to Stirner."

"So you believe the potential benefits outweigh the risks?"

"Yeah."

"How far his talents go will depend on how well you command him."

"I'm aware of that."

"Remember, Vincent; you are no longer a soldier in the field. Put the warrior aside and expand your mind. Your realm of influence has vastly expanded, and shortsightedness will be the end of you. Always think multiple steps ahead. You must adapt quickly. As we all must."

"I will," said Scheffler. "You have my word."

Kalakia turned and walked toward the study.

"Come," he said.

Inside Kalakia stood facing the world map on the wall, and Scheffler joined him.

"The battlefield is changing rapidly," said Kalakia.

"I know," said Scheffler. "I feel like we're walking on quicksand."

"You said earlier that we must regroup. What did you mean?"

"I don't know exactly. Last night while we were in the thick of it, I thought back on my time in Kosovo. We were caught in the forest, and the area was crawling with hostile soldiers. We had no idea of numbers or what their position would be at a particular point. Time was running out, and we had to extract our target. I solved the issue by laying charges in one direction and going another way. It worked. The enemy took the bait. You weren't wrong before. I'm not a soldier anymore, but all I see on this map is one enormous battlefield. War is war, regardless of the scale. Why not use the same tactics?"

"Are you suggesting misdirection?"

"That's right. We've been approaching this all wrong. When you're a hammer everything looks like a nail, right? We've been dominant for too long. We forgot what it's like to play chess."

"And how exactly will chess help us in this situation?" said Kalakia.

"I'm not sure. If we're using that analogy then I guess we need to focus on the centre squares and try to take the initiative. Can't see how attacking helped us yesterday though."

"What did last night teach you?"

"It taught me that we should never underestimate them again, that they're ready for a fight. That if we keep going down this road it's going to get ugly, and a lot of innocent people are going to die."

"You believe we can avoid this fate?"

Scheffler exhaled and rubbed his chin.

"I don't know," he said. "It's a tough situation. Morale is as low as I've ever seen it. The soldiers think you've lost your magic. That you don't have a plan to beat these guys. They're worried."

"And what is your opinion? Have I lost my magic?"

"No way," said Scheffler quickly, shaking his head. "You're still you. Doesn't mean you're not human, though. I'd understand if you're feeling the pinch."

Kalakia did not speak for a long time.

"Thank you, Vincent," he finally said. "That will be all."

"Right," said Scheffler, clearing his throat.

Scheffler hesitated, almost saying something before turning and leaving the room, shutting the door behind him.

Kalakia remained staring at the map for some time then went over and sat behind his desk, resting his head on his knuckles while ruminating about what Scheffler had said.

He realised he had not eaten anything all day, having been unable to break through the nausea of the last forty-eight hours. He rubbed his temples to help ease the pressure in his head, then went into his bedroom to take a nap.

20

The headlights of the approaching police car lit up the street and quickly gave it away. It rolled by slowly, before Frederich emerged from his hiding spot behind a parked vehicle and continued creeping alongside the river, on his way to Vidrik's last known location. To his right stood a series of houseboats floating quietly in the early morning darkness. It was apparent the city was still in lockdown. The neighbourhood had an uncanny vibe, as though danger could lie waiting around any corner. Frederich was glazed with sweat and the veins in his neck were throbbing. The leaves of the trees rustled briefly in the wind as he felt his surroundings with agonising sensitivity, every nearby crack or shuffle sending aftershocks through his entire body. He continued another block with the knowledge that a bullet could come from anywhere. The trees and houseboats became potential harbingers of death, along with every parked car that he approached.

The sight of Vidrik standing a block away underneath a streetlight took him by surprise. *What the hell?* He froze like a deer, while his hand reached automatically for his pistol before Vidrik disappeared around the corner. With his gun drawn, Frederich ducked close to the ground and rushed forward. At the corner he listened carefully before tip-toeing around and looking down a narrow, empty road. Street lights, parked cars and trees dominated the entire length, making it well-lit yet full of hiding places. He hesitated, sensing something dubious, then decided against giving chase. It was an obvious trap.

A shadow moved at the far end of the street and disappeared to the right. Frederich stood biting his lip. *What game are you playing, Vidrik?* He jogged forward, holding his pistol ready at the side. Moments later a loud blast shook him stiff, with three bullets fired in quick succession. He hesitated, then broke out in a sprint. At the next corner he took shelter behind a parked car and looked out at a modern, four-storey apartment block with full-length glass balconies and large windows. The lights in the surrounding apartments were coming on one by one, and the apartment on the first level had a smashed balcony and window. Frederich scrunched his nose and checked the street ahead. There was no sign of Vidrik, and his senses told him Vidrik was already gone. He took off, running past the apartment block, catching glances from the concerned inhabitants who were staring out sheepishly from behind their curtains.

Every street looked identical. If Frederich reached an intersection, he instinctively chose a direction while trying to anticipate the next dramatic clue in Vidrik's odd game. It came moments later behind him in the form of an angry yell along with the crack of two more bullets. He flipped around and ran the length of the street, pointing his pistol forward as he turned in the direction of where the sound came. Waiting for him was a police car in the middle of the road with the driver's door wide open. A policeman was lying in his navy-blue uniform on the asphalt in a bloody mess. He was not moving. Frederich studied the area for a moment then approached and found the policeman with a bullet in his chest and skull. Frederich shook his head furiously. Vidrik was starting to get on his nerves. No way Frederich was turning back, but he was reluctant to play along with whatever the hell Vidrik was doing. There was no time for a debate. He pressed on while being watched by dozens more frightened onlookers from their apartments. This time he tossed the cautious approach aside and picked up the pace.

The longer he worked his way through the labyrinth of streets, the more hot and bothered he felt. He frantically sought out a solution, for a way to one-up Vidrik and get the jump on him. Nothing came to mind. Frederich only felt a prickly irritation passing over his skin. It thrust him forward, convincing him that when the time came, he would know what to do. Meanwhile, his breathing grew shallower and his focus scattered. He stopped following his intuition and took random turns instead, hoping to catch Vidrik off-guard, praying for some luck.

Another bullet was fired. He sprinted in its direction, first thinking he might have taken a wrong turn when the sound of a man's piercing scream from an apartment block ahead dispelled his doubt. Vidrik disappeared behind a tree at the far end of the street before another, more hysterical scream filled the neighbourhood. Frederich approached the apartment block from the road and found a man in the living room of the bottom-floor apartment, dressed in shorts and a t-shirt, looking down over a dead body. The man had his trembling arms held out and was sobbing with a look of disbelief. Vidrik had shot and killed someone through his front window. Frederich shut his eyes for a second and clenched his fists. Then another bullet fired in the distance caused him to jerk involuntarily.

"Ah!" he screamed in frustration.

He took off again, his breathing rapid and out of control, his eyes stinging from the profuse sweat dripping down his forehead. The street became a blurry tunnel which descended into a strange, nauseating hell. Kraas' voice blared in Frederich's head, urging him to slow down and weigh his next step. *Forget it.* A car would be helpful, he realised. A thought crossed his mind to go back and force the surviving man to hand over his keys. He ignored it. With his pistol raised, he ran out onto a major t-intersection with a tree-filled park across the road. It was a dead-end, unless Vidrik had gone inside the park? Frederich stood out in the open and aimed erratically in every direction, furiously searching the area for any sign of danger. *Where the hell is he!?* There was another gun blast behind him. He raced back the way he came, struggling to draw air into his lungs. Back at the same apartment, he carefully searched the area around him. Then he glanced through the shattered window inside the living room. The man from earlier was no longer in sight. Frederich was on the opposite footpath, and went around a parked car and crossed the road. Once he approached the fence, he looked over and found that there were two dead bodies now. His eyes lit wide-open, his chest began heaving as he came close to hyperventilating.

"Vidrik!!" he screamed, raising his head to the sky.

There was a hint of the rising sun when an approaching police siren came blaring from the other street. Frederich grasped his pistol tight and marched off in its direction. He turned the corner and heard the voices of two men yelling something in French, followed by two more gun blasts. He followed the winding road with his gun pointed forward, his finger aching to pull the trigger. On a footpath which ran off the street and between two apartment blocks was a Peugeot police car, standing at an angle with both doors open and the siren lights still blinking. Frederich approached from behind, using the vehicle for shelter and aiming forward. One policeman's body was lying still on the grass to his left. Another policeman was sitting up in the front doorway to one of the apartment blocks, still alive but nursing a stomach wound. Frederich quickly turned his pistol in the opposite direction. The grass-covered opening between the buildings was as big as a football field. There were large trees and bushes randomly scattered among crisscrossing footpaths. Vidrik was still out there. Frederich was sure of it. He aimed his pistol erratically between every possible hiding spot. A gun went off again from among some bushes, and Frederich immediately fired two shots in that general direction. *Dammit.* He had to be careful; a stray bullet could make its away into one of the ground floor apartments.

The policeman in the doorway was dead. Frederich knew that without needing to look. His vision grew foggy, made worse by his shallow breathing. He searched frantically, but saw no trace of Vidrik. If he moved from his position, he would be exposed. The void was now pressing up against him, ready to welcome him if he wanted. Every inch of his body was screaming at him to go out there, to meet Vidrik head-on and — if need be — to die in a glorious, bloody mess. Holding him back was a sick sense of pride, a refusal to let Vidrik have the last laugh. Ida's battered face came to the forefront of his mind, as did her words: 'So come back.' It instilled in him an immense desire to come out on top. How would he achieve that victory? *Think, Frederich!* Then it occurred to him. His body was resting on it.

He lowered his gun and ducked, then crawled to the passenger side of the Peugeot. He slid inside, shuffling over to the driver's seat. The keys were not in the hole. He thought hard, refusing to abandon the idea. It was all he had. Then he looked to his side and saw the keys on the grass. They must have fallen out of the policeman's hands as he scrambled after Vidrik. The driver's door was wide open, and would provide Frederich with some shelter. It was worth the risk, but he would have to be quick. He took a deep breath and reached his arm out, quickly ducking his head out and snatching the keys from the grass. Once he was seated with his head lowered and the key was in the hole, he switched on the ignition. Vidrik immediately fired at him, opening a large crack in the windshield. The second shot hit the side of the car with a clang before Frederich put the car into gear. He kept his head low and pressed on the accelerator, randomly veering left and right to make Vidrik's aim lousier. He made a loop around a set of bushes and found nothing. As he made his way to the next bush, Vidrik finally emerged and began sprinting in the opposite direction. Frederich floored it, quickly gaining ground until he was forced to hit the brakes when Vidrik veered around a tree. The car came sliding to a halt before Frederich grasped his pistol. By then Vidrik had disappeared through an opening between two buildings. Frederich heard the sound of sirens coming from the street. He looked behind him, and the hairs on his head lifted. Four police cars came racing over the grass. Turning forward again, he realised the distance to the opening that Vidrik had taken was too far away.

The police cars screeched to a halt. Option one was to switch on the engine again, but there was no space to manoeuvre his way out. Option two was to make a run for it. Option three was to fight. As he made his decision, police officers began flooding out of their cars. He got out of the vehicle, taking a sidewards glance as he rushed off. Numerous guns were pointed in his direction, and a flurry of furious yells came his way. He sprinted around the tree, using its thick trunk as a shield. The first shots rang, causing explosions of dirt to fly up on either side of him. The tree would offer no protection during the final stretch. He jumped for it, somersaulting through the final metres as he crossed through the gap. He made it, but not without some damage as he hit the concrete. The adrenaline shot through him like a rapid river, and he rose to his feet to escape before collapsing back to the ground. Had he broken a bone when he fell? He looked down and saw drops of blood across the ground, with a splatter of it beneath him. A buzzing feeling emerged in his thigh while numbness washed over him. *Oh, no.* Just as he realised he had been shot, the police officers emerged from around the corner, rushing forward with guns pointed while screaming loudly at him in French. One of them kicked his pistol away then forced him to his stomach, pulling his arms back and handcuffing him. It was then that the bullet hole erupted, a piercing, scorching sensation spreading through his leg like wildfire.

21

Ida came back down to Earth with a thud, the jet blasting over the Tegel Airport runway before the backward thrust of the brakes slowed it to a crawl. Ida had been staring vacantly ahead and mindlessly flicking between songs on her phone. Even her favourite tracks lacked appeal, and she eventually shut it off and tucked her headphones into her handbag before sitting up and staring impatiently at the front of the plane, suddenly desperate to escape her seat.

Disembarking was agony. Ida clenched her teeth, seething in the stale air of the cabin while watching the people clumsily struggle with their bags in the compartments above. *Hurry up, idiots.* When she finally shuffled through the tight aisle and emerged onto the runway, the fresh air gave her little comfort. She entered the terminal and carried her bag up the stairs before rolling it toward the exit, passing by the baggage carousel. Outside she ignored the buses and marched toward the taxi rank instead. While leaving the airport, she responded with one-word answers to the driver's attempts at discussing her injuries and the terror of the previous night, before closing her eyes for the rest of the ride when he got that she did not want to talk.

Back in Neukölln, she stood briefly on the sidewalk watching Berliners rushing past, too absorbed in themselves to notice her. The injuries on her face. Her frown which made her chin feel tight. Her absence of spirit.

She opened the door to her building and lumbered upstairs with her suitcase. She left everything by the door and got undressed in the living room, tossing her clothes on the sofa. She filled a glass of water in the kitchen and took a long sip on the way to the bedroom, leaving the cup on her side table. The sheets on the bed were clean. She always changed them with fresh ones before going away somewhere, since it made coming home that much sweeter. Today it made no difference to her. She crawled in, covering most of her head and rolling onto her stomach, the mattress and thick blanket cradling her to sleep.

Are you back?? Tell me you're ok? read Chi's message; the first thing Ida saw when she woke at 2:17 pm.

The fourteen hours of sleep had done her some good. A gentle, glowing ember warmed her stomach from inside, and caused tingles over her skin as she breathed deeply into it. She rolled off the bed and went to the bathroom, having a warm shower while trying to avoid aggravating her cuts and bruises. A steaming bowl of oats in her lap, she sat on the sofa and stared into space while her mind meditated on Paris.

She had been half-walking, half-jogging along the bridge, nervously checking for Vidrik, when a police car pulled up behind her. The window rolled down, and a woman yelled something out at her in French. Ida stopped and shook her head to indicate she did not understand.

"What are you doing?" asked the police officer, this time in English. She had a light brown ponytail, big brown eyes and a wide mouth. "It is not safe to be out here."

Once the woman noticed the state of Ida's face her hardened expression changed. She got out and gently guided Ida into the backseat without saying another word. They drove to the hospital in silence, and a distracted looking, silver-haired doctor in his sixties tended to Ida's wounds. He cleaned the gash above her eye and stitched it up while she held an ice pack against her stomach. He then placed a tiny bandage over her cut and after inspecting her ribs advised her that they were bruised but not broken. They would heal soon, and she should avoid lifting heavy objects or doing anything strenuous in the following weeks. Finally, he handed her a tiny pack of painkillers and rushed out of the room.

Olivia, the police officer who had helped Ida into the police car, explained that the chaos in the city had stretched the hospital's resources as well as the police's. She moved Ida to an empty doctor's office and prepared to take a statement. Ida froze, her mind scrambling to decide how much she should divulge. Elias, Frederich, The League. There was too much to tell, and going down that path would only complicate her life. She kept it simple. She had been invited to a cocktail party by a fashion agent. She was looking for a taxi to go home when she heard the gunshots in the distance and realised when the streets were empty that something was wrong. On her way through the esplanade a man stalked and attacked her, and she eventually fought him off. When asked what the man looked like, she decided there was no harm in describing Vidrik as he was. Olivia asked why Ida did not go back inside the party when she heard the gunshots. Ida froze for a second, cleared her throat, then said she was already too far away, and the man had blocked her path back. Olivia appeared unsatisfied by Ida's story but did not press her. She checked the time then rubbed her weary eyes before stating that Ida could fly home immediately if she wished. The police might need to contact her again at some stage when the situation calmed down.

It was a relief to be back in Berlin. Ida finished her last spoonful of oats then picked up her phone. She replied: *Yes, I'm back. And I'm ok. Can we meet today?*

By the time she got dressed Chi had written back.

Of course! I'm working remotely. Come down, wrote Chi, attaching a pinned location on Pannierstrasse just around the corner.

Ida grabbed her handbag and left the apartment. She stepped out into the sun, taking a moment to absorb its uplifting effect before tilting her head and looking around. She had been too exhausted to notice last night, but now in the bright afternoon light it was unmistakable.

The people looked afraid.

Two young men stood at the street corner chatting. They had smiles on their faces, but their eyes were darting around. A family of five walked by, followed closely by two women. The mother of the family stopped suddenly, appearing indecisive about which direction to take next, and the two women nearly bumped into her, flinching and stepping back in the process. They all held out their hands and apologised profusely to each other with intense stares. A man dragged his luggage down the path with his head down and with no regard for those around him. Another man waited at the crossing with his girlfriend, rubbing his neck and looking around nervously. Ida wrinkled her nose and began moving down the walkway with slow steps, cautiously navigating her way through the fear in the air, careful not to disturb the odd, fragile equilibrium in the neighbourhood.

She turned the corner onto Pannierstrasse and approached the cafe where Chi was sitting, finding her outside with a cup of coffee. Chi had her laptop open and was staring earnestly at the screen while rubbing her wrist, totally absorbed in what she was reading.

"Hey," said Ida after standing by the table for some time.

Chi cowered and gasped at the same time, looking up at Ida with a disturbed expression before growing calm when she realised who it was.

"Hey," she said, her face blushing. "Sorry, I was just…" She looked carefully at Ida's face. "What the hell happened to you?" she said, standing up suddenly.

"Oh," said Ida, rubbing the bandage above her eye. "Don't worry, I'm fine."

"Yeah, but what happened?"

Chi reached out but resisted the temptation to touch Ida's bruised face, biting her bottom lip as she looked over the wounds.

Ida did not want to get into a long-winded explanation. She just wanted a friend, someone whose presence would tell her that everything was going to be ok. Chi locked eyes with her, and Ida began frowning. Her eyes slowly watered up.

"Oh," said Chi, pouting her lips and reaching over to pull her in. Ida rested her head on Chi and let herself be held. For a moment the street noise faded away, and the pain in her ribs disappeared.

"Sit down," said Chi. "I'll get you a drink of water. Do you want a coffee?"

Ida nodded, taking care with her ribs as she eased into the chair. A moment later Chi came back with a glass and sat down beside her.

"I guess I don't need to ask you how Paris was?" said Chi with a half-smile and look of concern.

"You were right," said Ida. "I shouldn't have gone."

"Oh, shut up," said Chi, waving her hand dismissively.

"No, I was an idiot," said Ida. "I need to learn to be more patient."

"I'm just glad you're ok. Did you get caught up in those attacks?"

"No," said Ida, shaking her head. "But I heard them from where I was."

"Then how did you get… that," said Chi, signalling at Ida's wounds.

"It's a long story," said Ida.

"Look," said Chi, pausing while her face turned serious. "You've been keeping secrets the whole time I've known you. I didn't say anything before because I didn't want to be nosey. I figured you had your reasons. But now it's gone too far. You need to tell me what's going on with you."

Ida gazed dumbfounded at Chi.

"To be honest, it's been getting on my nerves," continued Chi. "I can't just play stupid anymore. Not if your life's at risk."

Ida exhaled slowly.

"I didn't want to tell you because it might put you in danger," she said.

"Me?" said Chi, turning her head. "How?"

Ida shook her head and turned away.

"Ida, have you seen the news?" said Chi. "We're all in danger. The Chancellor is playing it all cool, telling us not to panic, but people aren't stupid. Everyone knows something big is brewing, and that it's probably going to get worse."

Ida turned back to Chi, whose determination was on full display. It was hard to admire her resolve while it was directed Ida's way, but she did have a point. The attacks had raised the stakes for the entire globe. The way Frederich had said 'war' foreshadowed what was to come. Ida had spent the last day trying to push apocalyptic thoughts out of her mind, but the unease was all around her. It was in the eyes of everyone she saw from Paris to Berlin. There was no sense in keeping Chi in the dark any longer.

"It started with a guy I met when I first came to Berlin," Ida said. "His name was Elias."

She only paused her story when the coffee came, and her cup was empty by the time she finished speaking. Chi had been listening intently, wholly immersed by what sounded like an elaborate piece of fiction. When Ida finished, they sat in silence for a long time, the weight of her harrowing tale hanging heavy over the two of them. Finally, Chi snickered and shook her head.

"That's intense. Really intense," she said, her eyes opening wide and crossing over each other. "Now I can see why you were so wound up."

Ida shrugged and smiled bashfully.

"This Vidrik guy sounds like a lunatic," said Chi.

"He is," said Ida.

"You go!" blurted Chi. "I'm so proud of you, taking him on like that."

"Frederich saved me," said Ida.

"Oh, don't give me that," said Chi. "You fought him yourself. And you probably saved that guy's life, the one from the party."

"Terence."

"Right. You could have kept him around to protect you. I know I would have, instead of facing that psycho all by myself."

Ida stared at the table, only able to think of Vidrik's first victim sprawled dead on the front steps of her building.

"I knew there was something about that Frederich guy," said Chi. "He kills people?"

Ida nodded, signalling to Chi to keep her voice down.

"Sorry," whispered Chi. "Excuse me for being worked up about all this."

Ida sighed, relieved that her secret was out, while suddenly overwhelmed by the state of society. How did things get so crazy? She thought about women like Olivia, who daily found the strength to face the ugliness of the world. Olivia looked exhausted by the events of the night, but her small, muscular frame remained upright, and she found a way to steel herself before leaving the room to face her next challenge. Ida had been shaken to her core by recent events, but she promised herself she would never let other people's wickedness get the best of her. The world was in conflict, and she could not control it. But just like Olivia, she would do her best to stay courageous. In Ida's mind, Frederich and Olivia stood on opposite sides of the spectrum of good and evil, but she remained awestruck by their capacity to persevere regardless of what difficulties they faced. Her own courage was still in its infancy, but she sensed it growing stronger each day, eclipsing that other feeling she was unable to shake. She looked at Chi.

"I'm scared," she said.

Chi nodded solemnly.

"I'm glad you said that," she said. "I am too. My first thought when this all happened was to go home, but this thing is global. There's nowhere we can hide. What are we going to do?"

Ida recalled the resolve in Frederich's face as he prepared to go after Vidrik, knowing he might be walking toward certain death.

"We're going to be brave," she said, sitting up in her chair. "We've got no other choice."

22

Frederich's pulse had slowed to a mild, muffled drum beat. The drug-induced lethargy had sapped him of his vigour, leaving his body limp and impotent. He forced his dense eyelids open and saw her again, standing next to a male doctor while pointing at a clipboard and signalling toward the door. She spoke quickly, her voice only a quiet mumble to Frederich, while the other doctor nodded earnestly before pushing the clipboard under his arm and leaving the room.

She stood thinking for a moment, draped in her white coat. She was a firm-bodied woman in her late fifties with greying brown hair tied into a bun. The way she stood there with steady conviction gave away her high position in the hospital. The defiant weariness in her face showed that she took her job seriously. Her attention suddenly turned to Frederich. She strode toward him then looked down with narrowed, curious eyes. He tried to speak but struggled to find the willpower. Voices approached from outside, and her head turned quickly toward the doorway. Without hesitating she reached over and promptly picked up a syringe and bottle. She was efficient, seamlessly drawing in the liquid and checking for air pockets as though she had done it a thousand times before. Frederich knew what was about to happen.

"No," he croaked, not wanting to go under again.

She turned her ear toward the door, her eyes lighting up.

"Please," he said, managing to find his voice. "Don't—"

The injection spread through his veins, neutralising any resistance he had been able to conjure. The intensity of the fluorescent light above grew blinding, and the doctor's face became a blur.

"Close your eyes," she said, gently placing her hand over his face.

A shadow appeared at the door, and a muffled conversation broke out as Frederich's eyelids fell shut. The pressure of the bed dissolved from beneath him while he lost all feeling. He entered a trance-like state, barely able to cling to consciousness. Then came the flashbacks from the other night in Bromley. He felt Pistol's body pressing up against his before it tumbled to the ground. Dikka's bulging eyes gaped at him, begging him not to attack. Faust's punches came his way, and his body convulsed trying to dodge them. Vent's grunting reverberated while he made his final gasp with his throat bloodied. The four men then wheezed collectively, united in death, their voices filling the black space before silence returned. Frederich welcomed it as he sunk deeper into the bed, until he became suspended in emptiness.

The image of the doctor's earthy, weathered face emerged, with wrinkles running across her forehead and her cheeks sagging at the side. Frederich's only remaining connection to his body was a dull ache in his chest. He felt drawn to the source of pain coming through the ache. At first the thought of going in there horrified him, until he returned his attention to her face. He knew at that moment that she had seen it all. He had no idea where that knowledge came from. He simply knew it to be true. Ages of suffering were imprinted on her face. Her eyes were steady, full of grief, but also gentle and kind. Her gaze was enough to reassure him to go inside. She smiled and nodded lightly, and he stopped resisting, allowing himself to drift until everything turned black.

Where am I? He floated effortlessly through the dark with nothing upon which to anchor himself. Immersed in the serenity which had flooded his consciousness, he descended a timeless, formless tunnel with a kind of ease he never thought possible. On he drifted, for what could have been hours, or mere seconds. He had no idea. He did not care. The tranquillity was everything, cuddling and nurturing him.

The shift away from the benevolent warmth was gradual — and ominous. A harsh chill began to seep in. *No.* He scrambled to go back, but had no way to influence the slow, unrelenting current. The emptiness no longer felt welcoming, but had transitioned into a cruel and caustic wilderness. *Let me out!* A huff of mist shot through the air. A rapidly escalating heartbeat pounded from a distance. Another huff blew by, then another, in time with her rasping breath. Her bulging eyes stared desperately at him as she crawled over the dirt, a stream of blood running down her forehead. He stood helpless in the distance, paralysed, conscious of every detail around him. The contours of the bark over the tree trunks, the icy breeze, the cooing of the birds, the moonlight reflecting off her knotted hair. His fingers trembled mercilessly while he maintained absolute eye contact with her. It was all he had to sustain him. If he looked away, it would be the end of him. The man's shadow emerged over her — the one who did all of this — and her breathing halted, her eyes swelling like a rising sun, illuminated by terror.

"Run!" she shrieked, her scream sending shockwaves over the landscape.

He ceased to exist. All that remained of him was a ball of fire, blinding in its intensity, horrific in its magnitude. It was unfathomable. Was he in hell? He had to be. When he returned he found himself sprinting through the forest, gasping for air. He halted suddenly, his bare feet kicking up dirt and dead leaves. The bear had come from nowhere, its massive, fearsome body dwarfing him as it rose on its hind legs. He turned to escape, before a hefty weight fell on him, forcing him to the ground while shredding the flesh of his back.

It was enough to force him awake. His torso sprung up from the hospital bed, sending a sharp pain through his wounded leg. He groaned and clutched at his bandage.

The room was dark, with only a tiny bit of light coming through the crack of the curtain. A hand touched his shoulder. He turned suddenly and saw her, the doctor who had put him under.

"Shh," she said, raising her index finger to her mouth. "Be quiet."

Frederich tried to fix his gaze on her, drowsy from the morphine, still shook up by his nightmare. He took a deep breath and finally managed to make out the details of her face in the dark. His mouth and lips were parched, his body felt frail.

"Can I—"

"Keep your voice down," she interjected with a heavy French accent. "They can hear."

Frederich shook his head and blinked multiple times.

"Can I have water?" he whispered.

"Yes," she whispered back.

She reached over to the table by the side.

"Lie down," she whispered. "If the door opens, close your eyes."

"Why?" he said, lowering his head to the pillow again.

"They want to take you from here. I told them you have an infection which threatens your life, and that I need to stay with you."

"I don't understand," he whispered.

"I believe they want to harm you."

"Is that why you put me to sleep again?"

"Yes, I'm sorry. They were outside. If they saw you awake, they may have taken you."

Frederich thought hard. *They?* If The League had sent them, then she was wasting her time. This woman seemed savvy enough to sense danger, however, and he decided he would trust her. He nodded his acceptance.

She put a plastic cup to his mouth. He reached his hands up and took it, slowly drinking all of the water, then handed the cup back. She turned her ears to the door briefly, then turned back to Frederich, seeming satisfied that there was no immediate danger outside. She gave Frederich a weary smile.

"Thank you," he said. "For helping me."

She nodded, looking pale and exhausted. Frederich had important questions for her, but could not ignore the look on her face.

"Are you ok?" he asked.

"Hmm?" she said. "Yes. It's been a hard day."

"What happened?"

She pursed her lips and shook her head dismissively. Frederich kept his eyes on her and waited.

"A man came in yesterday with serious head trauma," she said. "He was severely beaten. We stabilised him. I don't know what went wrong. He was fine when I left. We lost him some hours ago."

Frederich silently watched her fighting with her anguish, as she alternated between near tears to stiff resistance. He had no idea how to respond. A lump emerged in his throat, and his stomach began turning. He thought for a moment. The man was probably one of The League's targets. If so, then good riddance.

She exhaled loudly.

"There was just too much death," she said.

Frederich's stomach continued to turn. He cleared his throat, but it remained lumpy.

"Why are you helping me?" he asked.

She gave him a blank stare, as though not knowing how to answer the question.

"They told you why they arrested me?" he asked.

She nodded.

"You committed murder," she said.

When the police turned up, Vidrik was already out of sight. All they had was a trail of dead bodies and Frederich sitting metres away in a police car with a gun. He had not killed the people they would be accusing him of. But she was still right. He had committed murder before.

"Why are you helping me?" he said again, growing more uneasy.

"The Paris police are very angry with you. You killed their friends. I don't know what they would do if I let them take you."

"If I did kill their friends, why does it matter?"

She tilted her head as though confused by his logic.

"You are speaking of an eye for an eye?"

He nodded.

"You don't value your life?" she said. "You don't value the life of others?"

Her question was like a jolt of high-voltage electricity which hit Frederich in the gut. Her grave stare cut through the darkness and penetrated him. He felt his face burn up and he turned away. There were no simple answers. Of course it was her job to blindly save lives. Did she not understand that evil did not negotiate? That it was evil which did not value the lives of others. *Idealist. She can't help it.*

"What do they look like?" he asked, turning back with newly-found defiance.

"Who?"

"The policemen who want to take me."

"They have brown hair. One has a moustache. They take turns guarding the room. Do you want to kill them?"

Frederich bit his lower lip. He shook his head.

"I just want to know who's after me."

"There is another man. He came asking questions. He claimed to be your brother. I didn't trust him. I told him that we moved you to another hospital."

Frederich frowned and stared expectantly at the doctor.

"He had a round face, strange eyes."

Vidrik.

"And long black hair," she added.

Frederich tilted his head.

"The hair is a disguise," he said.

"You know him?"

"Yes."

"Is he dangerous?"

"Very."

They had gone down a rabbit hole for which the doctor was not prepared. She now looked ten years older, the stress finally getting the better of her.

"You've done too much for me," said Frederich. "You should go. I'll be fine."

She closed her eyes and shook her head.

"No," she said, opening her eyes again. "This is my unit. And you are my patient."

Frederich snickered and shook his head. *Definitely an idealist.*

She moved back into the dark, returning to her chair in the corner where Frederich could hear her breath. He began to consider a plan to get out of this fix. It did not look good. He had been shot in the leg, and he was trapped in a hospital room guarded by a furious policeman who thought he had killed innocent people, including a number of fellow officers. As if that were not bad enough, Vidrik was somewhere out there. Even with no legs, Frederich could take care of a police officer. Getting out would be another issue. Taking on Vidrik on top of that meant he would need to innovate his plans beyond using force. Should he wait it out? Or should he call for help? There were no clear answers. For now he was still alive, and for that he could thank... her.

"What's your name?" he whispered through the darkness.

"Camille," she said.

"I'm Frederich."

The room went silent. When she still said nothing, Frederich assumed she wanted to sleep. She had looked exhausted enough.

"Goodnight," he said, assuming she was already out.

There was another long pause before her voice suddenly came from the corner.

"Goodnight, Frederich," she said.

23

Inselheim and the Neutralaser team were back in action.

The semi-trailer truck sent out beep after screeching beep as it slowly reversed through the roller door. The side of the sixty-foot long container was decorated from top to bottom with an enormous illustration of a green apple and the business name beneath it. On the road from the mansion, Inselheim had noticed they were in a fruit-growing region. Now it made sense. A fruit company was an excellent cover strategy to get the equipment shipped in without suspicion.

The warehouse itself was beneath Inselheim's typical standards. He kicked his heel into the dust-covered concrete floor, exposing the many months the place had remained unused. He inspected the vintage brickwork, the paint on the window sills which was now peeling off. The air was heavy with the residual smell of chemicals. The building itself was vastly smaller than their now destroyed state-of-the-art facility in Kazakhstan, and the equipment at their disposal was nowhere near as cutting edge. Still, it was better than nothing. The Neutralaser team was at least safe and able to work.

Ignoring the chemical stink, Inselheim inhaled deeply and smiled. There was no sign of his panic attacks. He had slept all through the previous nights, a feat he had not achieved in a long time. The team was shuffling around organising the space, and the scene reminded him of the first days of the Neutralaser project. Shirvan was busy directing the forklift driver where to place the crates. Phil and Mona exchanged smiles while putting together the work desks for the design department. The manufacturing team were in deep discussion about how to arrange the robotics equipment. Brunswick was hunched over her computer terminal in the corner.

"You would think The League of Reckoning never existed," said Inselheim as he approached. "The way everyone is back at work."

He noticed the Neutralaser blueprints on her screen.

"Hmm?" said Brunswick, half turning to Inselheim while still absorbed in her work.

"The team," said Inselheim, taking a seat next to her. "It's good to see them."

"They've been through a lot," said Brunswick, her attention now shifting to him.

"So have you," said Inselheim.

"We all have," replied Brunswick with a stern nod.

"I spoke to some of the team. They told me you were amazing. They think they wouldn't have made it without you."

"I did what I had to," said Brunswick.

"Well, you did good," said Inselheim. "I know it wasn't easy."

Brunswick went silent, her stare turning vacant, which reminded Inselheim of how much the past months had fundamentally changed her. On the surface she was still her tenacious self, but when Inselheim searched deeper there was a part of her which, previously accessible to him, was now locked shut. The soft edges of her personality were gone. Nobody discussed what had happened, and the team loyally followed Brunswick's lead in going straight back to work. Inselheim wondered if they would show symptoms of trauma as he had, but he did not dare open his mouth. The team was likely dealing with the fall-out of their ordeal in their own way. In Inselheim's case, it was after sunset that the nightmares began, when the distraction of work was left behind. For now, he would play along, glad to have rediscovered some order in the chaos.

"Everything there?" he asked, signalling to the blueprints.

Brunswick re-gathered her focus.

"Yes, I'm just preparing the file system for Phil and the others."

"Great," said Inselheim.

"Whose genius idea was it to keep remote backups again?" said Brunswick.

Inselheim snickered and shook his head. They had debated for a long time the security implications of using an external server in Norway. Inselheim had been anxious about vulnerability to hackers, Brunswick had voiced her concerns about keeping everything in-house, which left the risk of losing their precious data too high for comfort.

"You do think of everything," he said. "Did I mention I'm glad to have you back?"

"A hundred times," said Brunswick. "I missed you too."

Inselheim knew she meant it, but her words lacked the usual warmth to which he was accustomed. *Give her time.*

"Kimberley?" came a voice from behind.

Inselheim and Brunswick turned around and saw Mona approaching.

"One second, Michael," said Brunswick and got up.

Inselheim watched Brunswick and Mona together from a distance. They communicated with ease, seamlessly laying hands on each other as they spoke, nodding at the right times, their facial expressions perfectly synced. Inselheim could only imagine what they had gone through together, but the effect had been powerful. Brunswick had grown more determined, more imposing, and her presence among the team was like an army general among their troops.

Heads suddenly turned toward the door as Stirner entered, flanked by three of his guards. Mona brushed her red hair out of her face and walked away, a small nod from Brunswick signalling the end of their meeting. Inselheim lifted himself off his chair, preparing himself to greet Stirner. Rather than approach Inselheim, Stirner went over to Brunswick instead. Inselheim stood in place, his cheeks growing progressively warmer as Stirner and Brunswick shared a long exchange without acknowledging him. Finally, Stirner and Brunswick finished their conversation and walked together toward Inselheim.

"Good afternoon, Michael," said Stirner.

"Horst. Hello," said Inselheim, stealing a glance at Brunswick, who looked somewhat foreign to him for a split second.

"So what do you think of the place?" said Stirner. "I hope it didn't disappoint you too much? Unfortunately, we need to prioritise safety over luxury. Kalakia's spies are difficult to elude."

"It'll do just fine for now," said Inselheim.

"Good sport," said Stirner, lightly slapping Inselheim's shoulder, which caused Inselheim to tense up.

The conversation fell flat, as Stirner smirked and shifted his gaze expectantly from Inselheim to Brunswick and then back.

"Ah, I see my people managed to get the blueprints to you," said Stirner, turning to the contents of the computer screen. "I know this is somewhat inconvenient, you not having access to telephone or the internet. I don't like treating you like my prisoners. I hope you understand."

"We understand very well," cut in Brunswick.

"Excellent," said Stirner. "We should see each other more as business partners. With some minor exceptions, of course."

"We can live with that," said Brunswick. "How about we set the guidelines now, to avoid confusion later?"

"What did you have in mind?" said Stirner, crossing his arms, his expression switching from quietly confident to cold neutrality.

"We can all agree that the team has been through a lot. I want a doctor made available round the clock, and I want the authority to decide who needs a break and when."

"Of course," said Stirner. "The health of your team is critical to our success. I'll have a doctor brought in. I'll also let you manage the work schedule, but know this; our enemies do not sleep. The situation could escalate rapidly, and I may ask more of you with little notice."

"Ok. Let's start with the doctor," said Brunswick. "Second, the Inselheim Group doesn't know if its CEO is dead or alive. Our shareholders will be getting nervous. The company is in enough trouble as it is. We want word sent out that he's ok."

"That could be difficult," said Stirner. "Any new information could trigger a search, which would complicate matters for me."

"I figured you would say that," said Brunswick. "And I have a solution."

"Yes?" said Stirner.

"You have ambitious plans. With the Neutralaser in your hand, nations will be forced to take you seriously."

"Correct," said Stirner.

"If we're going to be business partners, that should include The Inselheim Group. I want whatever pact you make with those nations to include an agreement to buy arms exclusively from us. You'll get your share, of course."

Wait, what? thought Inselheim, who had been passively listening to the exchange. Did she want to make the Inselheim Group the official weapons manufacturer of this guy's criminal organisation? *Say something.* Inselheim tried to open his mouth, but was held back by an emerging sense of helplessness.

"That's an interesting thought," said Stirner. "I'll think about it."

"You haven't heard everything," said Brunswick.

Stirner lifted his eyebrows in anticipation.

"The League Of Reckoning has a strong grip on world nations. Even with the Neutralaser, it won't be easy to convince all of them to shift their loyalty at once. They have too much at stake. Any sudden shift in alliance could prematurely trigger a nuclear war, and nobody wants that. It's more likely that they'll group up and send in their army to take the technology by force. You'll be vulnerable without a strong deterrence plan."

"I see you've thought hard about this," said Stirner with a tense smirk.

"But.." Brunswick paused, pursing her lips together, her expression darkening. "If we deployed the Neutralaser along with a set of long-range ballistic nuclear missiles, it would be a different story. Then they'll be forced to play along."

Nuclear missiles? Inselheim's legs suddenly grew weak as his helplessness deepened.

Stirner studied Brunswick's face for a long time.

"I don't have access to that kind of technology," he said.

"Leave that to me," said Brunswick.

Stirner stared silently at Brunswick, then finally broke out chuckling. It barely made a dent in the tension Brunswick had created.

"Amusing," said Stirner. "I have something much simpler planned. But I will keep your offer in mind, in case something changes."

"Do that," said Brunswick, maintaining absolute eye-contact.

"Now," said Stirner, blinking multiple times as though having woken up from hypnosis. "I'll be away for a couple of days. I trust you have everything you need in the meantime?"

"Yes," said Brunswick.

"I'll get that doctor sent over," said Stirner with a nod before walking away.

With Stirner gone, Inselheim was finally able to force words out of his mouth.

"Are you crazy?" he said. "Did I hear right? Nuclear missiles?"

Brunswick looked back at him with a hard, impenetrable stare.

"What do you want, Michael?" she said.

"What do you mean?"

"Do you want to succeed?"

"Yes. Of course," Inselheim said. "But you're talking about risking nuclear war. I want the opposite of that."

"We've known each other for a long time, haven't we?"

"Yes," said Inselheim. "But I don't think I know you very well right now. Something's changed."

"Of course it has," said Brunswick with a scowl. "That's the problem. The whole situation has changed, and you're still stuck in your fantasy world. What do you suggest we do? Tell me."

Inselheim took a deep breath.

"I think we should slow down," he said. "Consider what we're doing before it's too late."

"It's already too late," said Brunswick. "Your plan to make this technology and then magically deploy it worldwide without a hitch, that's never going to happen."

"It wasn't just my plan. It was *our* plan," said Inselheim.

"Didn't this whole experience with The League Of Reckoning teach you anything?" said Brunswick, now raising her voice. "Act, or be acted upon. Remember you used to say that? Well, we were acted on, and people died. Our friends were killed."

"You don't think that hurts me too?" said Inselheim.

"You weren't there locked up with us," said Brunswick.

"What is this really about?"

"It's about getting the job done. Stirner has his head so far up his ass he can't see what he's getting himself into. Kalakia is going to make breakfast out of him. Don't be the same. Don't let some bloated fantasy cut you off from reality."

"And what's the reality, Kimberley?"

"The reality is that the world isn't ready for this. We need to drag them kicking and screaming. If we don't, then everything we've worked for is gone."

"This is crazy," said Inselheim, placing his hands on the back his neck and shaking his head.

"We're a weapons manufacturer," said Brunswick. "We make money off products that kill people. Face it. Deep down you wanted to build the Neutralaser so you could feed your ego. It was your reputation you cared about, not the future of mankind. It was all about legacy for you. Don't be such a hypocrite."

Brunswick had delivered her last lines like a knockout punch, with such spite in her voice that Inselheim could not bring himself to hear any more. Her voice was like sandpaper tearing his insides to shreds, a corrosive liquid eating into his soul. He grew suddenly desperate to escape her laser-sharp stare. He stormed off, and fled to a corner behind the containers.

There he sat alone, dizzy with doubt and confusion. He stayed crouched on the ground for what felt like hours. Nobody came to check on him. After a short silence, the warehouse had broken into chatter again and the team seemed to get back to work. When Inselheim realised nobody was coming, he felt helpless and alone. What had just happened? Only this morning he had been filled with hope. Now his closest friend had turned his world upside-down. Being eviscerated like that by Brunswick was too much. Inselheim started sweating and shaking, as a new wave of panic attacks hit him, leaving him wondering when this nightmare was ever going to end.

24

Gerricks rubbed his eyes and turned from the screen, trying to blink away the soreness. The stream of information coming through was merciless. His shoulders and back were stiff like rock, his usually unwavering focus was failing him. A nap would have been a smart idea, but there was no time for that. The news was in a frenzy about the attacks, and rightfully so. There was no ignoring what had occurred in such a short time and on that kind of scale. The social media wheel was spinning like a jet engine. It was The Worldwide Horror all over again, and League Intel had long given up trying to control the narrative.

Gerricks reached over and grabbed his bottle of caffeine pills and shook two into his hand, tossed them into his mouth and washed them down with a gulp of energy drink. He managed to force his attention back to the screen, which showed #armageddon, #murder and #nowheretohide as the most trending hashtags in the world. Existential fear was collectively boiling up to the surface, uniting all people under the banner of impending doom. Web servers were dropping one-by-one from the sheer volume of users scampering to find ways to unload their angst via the web. Gerricks marvelled from his computer terminal at the reactions. A movement had begun planning for a migration north beyond the Nordic countries before 'World War III broke out.' Iceland was also mentioned in the discussion. Countless frightened citizens had crowded government offices all over the world. Sporadic incidents of looting had broken out. Supermarkets were quickly selling out of survival food. Protests were being planned in every nation to demand answers. *Good luck with that.*

Global stability might as well have been propped up with toothpicks, but Gerricks had his mind on something else. He sat ruminating about it until the caffeine pills kicked in, where his heart began pounding like a jackhammer and an involuntary shaking had taken over his legs. His neck cracked all over as he stretched it from side to side while trying to roll the tension out of his shoulders.

"I'm going for a walk," he told the team when his restlessness grew unbearable.

They acknowledged his comment with disinterested grunts without moving their eyes from the screens. Gerricks walked the length of the bunker and emerged out into the forest. He strode up the ramp then leaned against a tree and lit a cigarette, oblivious to the various signs of life in the woods. He had been with The League for eight years and had never experienced anything like this. There had been minor crises, such as the recession which led to a sharp increase in unemployment. There was also the 'Tech Mutiny' in Silicon Valley, where the CEOs of the most influential technology companies had hired mercenaries to resist The League. There were other minor situations peppered in between as well, but not once did doubt seep into Gerricks' mind. Kalakia took care of those situations as though he had been expecting them. Where was Kalakia's genius move now? What the hell was he waiting for? Gerricks hated even to think it, but if he had to guess, he would say that Kalakia

214

had no idea what he was doing. The man was likely biding his time, hoping his opponent would shoot himself in the foot or something. The League had its chance already, and it had blown it.

Gerricks finished his cigarette and flicked the butt onto the concrete before returning inside. When he approached the surveillance room, a head popped out of the doorway.

"There you are. Where the hell did you go?" said Xavier before his head disappeared back inside.

Gerricks entered and found the screens had been synchronised to display a single paused video, which showed the Seal of the President of the United States.

"What's this?" said Gerricks.

"The White House just released this," said Xavier. "It's doing the rounds on all the cable news networks and social media."

Xavier pressed play, and the rest of the surveillance team stopped what they were doing and watched. The president walked toward the podium while holding a piece of paper, and after taking a moment to gather himself, lifted his head and looked toward the camera with a determined gaze.

"Today, I address not only my fellow Americans, but the entire globe," he began, clearing his throat. "After the events earlier this week which struck almost every nation, the world needs answers. *We deserve* answers. I have spoken with our allies and other world leaders, and all have affirmed their commitment to order and justice for the global community. No nation which prides itself on the rule of law will tolerate such brazen violence on its streets. We are under no illusion. All of us are aware of past indiscretions and violent acts, not excluding the events known as The Worldwide Horror. Previously, we have tolerated such violence for the sake of maintaining peace and prosperity."

The president paused while staring grimly into the camera.

"Our tolerance can only go so far," he continued. "All peace-loving nations must now come together and present a united front against the terrorists who have instigated these heinous acts. In accordance with this, I and the other leaders of the G20 nations will be holding an emergency meeting tomorrow at 4:00 pm Eastern Standard Time in New York City. At this meeting, we will be studying the detailed reports of our intelligence agencies as well as discussing a collective plan of action. When we are done, we will reveal the identity of these terrorists, along with a plan to bring them to justice. Meanwhile, our competent military and local law enforcement will ensure security. I close my address by reassuring the world that lawlessness and unchecked violence will not be tolerated, nor will terrorism be permitted on our streets. On behalf of your leaders, I wish to assert our commitment to restoring order to our collective nations and the entire planet. And make no mistake; we will succeed in this endeavour. Thank you."

The president finished his address by leaving the podium and escaping into the back room without acknowledging the press, whose questions had immediately exploded into a shouting frenzy.

Gerricks and Xavier looked at each other as though seeing someone come back from the dead, neither of them knowing what to say, before Gerricks picked up the phone and hurried to call Scheffler.

"What do you mean he's not available to talk!?" screamed Scheffler, gripping the phone so tight he felt it bending beneath his fingers.

"Were my words not clear?" came Francois' voice.

"Your words were clear, Francois. But they don't make any sense! Didn't you see the president's address?"

"I did, and so did Kalakia."

"So where the hell is he? We need to respond while we have the chance."

"No," said Francois firmly. "Kalakia's instructions are to wait and *do nothing*. We'll contact you soon."

Scheffler was about to pop, unable to tolerate Francois' condescending nonchalance a second further.

"This is total bullshit!" he yelled, thumping his finger on the phone multiple times in frustration before the connection finally closed.

What happened to the days when a person could slam a phone shut, he thought? He tossed the handset onto the desk and began huffing and pacing around the room. He could scarcely believe it. They were in deep shit, and Kalakia had his head in the sand. Those slimy bastards in their government buildings had to be shown who was boss! The League needed to start rolling heads immediately.

Scheffler stood biting his lower lip with his hands on his hips. He looked down at the desk and spotted his phone, feeling the urge to smash it to pieces. He clenched his hand into a fist and raised it, ready to slam it down like a hammer. Then he stopped, growing suddenly relaxed and lightheaded as a calming energy flowed through his body like a cool breeze. He put the 'hammer' away, letting his arm fall to his side. Taking his frustration out on his phone would do no good.

Chess was an enigma to Scheffler. On the one hand, he enjoyed the rush of being locked in a strategic battle. On the other hand, the complicated nature of the game frustrated him. Whenever he was outplayed or could see no direct path to victory, he would quickly lose his patience.

That same feeling was plaguing him again. How were they going to navigate this damn situation? The only person capable of playing the game on such a high level was Kalakia, and he was off somewhere shitting bricks. Scheffler exhaled slowly before looking down at the desk like it was a chessboard and tried to recall the basics. First, spread out and go after the centre squares. The League had done that, taking the battle public to the middle of every major city. Next, have no fear in exchanging piece for piece if it gets you ahead. The League had lost enough pawns last night, but were they now at an advantage? Not from where Scheffler was standing. Also, never leave your pawns isolated. When Scheffler sensed his men vulnerable to needless death, he pulled them out, saving them to fight another day. Even Kalakia approved of that move. To top it all off, The League's 'King' now remained safe in his corner, out of sight, having 'castled' out of the way and allowing his opponent to destroy The Grand Luxus. It would be poetic indeed if Kalakia were actually laying low while waiting for the board to open up, where he could finally make his decisive strike.

Wait a minute. Scheffler's breathing stopped as his consciousness expanded, gifting him the insight to see it all. His head suddenly dropped.

"Son of a bitch," he said.

It all made sense. How had he missed it? He began shaking his head, stunned but also furious. Kalakia had been playing multiple moves ahead the whole time. The Five Eyes list, sending the volatile Abel after Drexler, the worldwide counter-attack. Kalakia knew precisely what he was doing. He had used turmoil as his chessboard, and now the pieces were perfectly set. To top it all off, he had told nobody.

"Son of a bitch," said Scheffler again.

25

Shrouded in darkness, Horst Stirner sat on a cushioned chair on the front porch while looking out into the yard of his remote cottage, carefully watching his men pat down his guest. There was a single street light at the front of the property which illuminated the entrance from the dirt road. Otherwise the surrounding area relied on the moonlight, with the only inhabitants being the local fauna, from hares to foxes to the pygmy shrew.

Footsteps shuffled across the gravel before a figure appeared and carefully climbed the steps.

"Hello, Charles," said Stirner, switching on a dim lamp, revealing head of the CIA Charles Burley, wearing his navy blue suit and burgundy tie.

Burley looked down briefly at Stirner with an unimpressed expression, his mouth turned into a frown and his bushy eyebrows pushed together.

"Horst," he said, before taking a seat on the only other chair on the porch. "I thought for a second we were having this meeting in the dark."

"How was your journey?" said Stirner.

"Uneventful," replied Burley. "The opposite of what we can expect after tomorrow's meeting in New York."

"Just be ready and follow our lead when he responds."

"He's taking his time," said Burley. "The president expected the blowback to come straight away."

"He's reluctant to make the same mistake again," said Stirner. "He knows he's dealing with a worthy opponent. I can anticipate his every move."

"It's almost too good to be true," said Burley.

"The advantages of doing business with me," said Stirner.

"Don't count your chickens, Horst. You know him better than anyone. He's a cunning son of a bitch."

"Nonsense," said Stirner. "Without me, he's nothing. He walked into my trap like a fool, and now he has no place to go. After tomorrow, public opinion will turn against him. The people are terrified. They don't want a war. They'll be begging us to get rid of him. He can't fight me, your coalition and the rest of the world, all at the same time. He'll be a pariah. The most wanted terrorist of all time. It's over for him."

"Let's hope so," said Burley.

"You need to stop worrying and start planning for a post-Kalakia world."

"We're anticipating the recession to hit straight away."

"So be it," said Stirner. "An economic reshuffle was never going to be painless. The boom will come quickly once we untangle the wealth from his web."

"He's going to lash out," said Burley. "Again, why he hasn't already is beyond me."

"Stop worrying. Remember, I have all the intelligence you need on The League. Its structures, movements, locations. Just follow our lead. Blame any flare-up on Kalakia, and let the media spin it as another step toward defeating the threat. Chaos is king. The more terrified the people are, the more they'll beg for blood. The League will be history in less than a year."

"The president wants to know your thoughts about what to do when we find him."

Stirner rested his fist over his mouth and looked away. His body tingled with ecstasy at the thought. Kalakia dead. *What a delightful picture.* With the king gone, the throne would be free for the taking. The Neutralaser would rewrite the geopolitical map and herald in a new global order — with Stirner at the helm.

"We shoot him like the dog he is," said Stirner. "Any trial could turn into a farce. He refused to hand himself in, we say. The battle was furious, and he perished in the crossfire. Deeply regrettable."

"I thought you'd say that," said Burley. "The president feels the same way."

"Of course he does. He's a smart man."

"Don't kiss our ass, Horst," said Burley.

"Charles, please watch that foul mouth," said Stirner, shaking his head. "We are businessmen here. Civility must be maintained."

Burley briefly checked his smartphone then pushed it back inside his jacket pocket.

"I need to get back soon," he said. "We've got a lot to prepare before tomorrow."

"Of course," said Stirner.

"We still have one thing to discuss."

"More concerns? Haven't I set your mind at ease?"

"There are some important people asking about their money," said Burley.

"Ah," said Stirner.

"How much?"

"Twenty percent," said Stirner. "Twenty percent of all the wealth in The League's possession. The rest I'll let you distribute as you see fit."

"We'll give you ten percent. Not a penny more."

"Good. So fifteen it is," said Stirner.

"*Ten* percent," said Burley. "Non-negotiable."

Stirner clenched his jaw. His anger boiled up, lifting him out of his chair as he fought it back. It took a moment for the wave to pass, as Burley's determined stare infuriated him, until finally he grew calm again. *Patience.* He nodded reluctantly in agreement, knowing that the real negotiation would begin when the guns started firing and the streets were littered with bodies.

"Right," said Burley. "So what do we need to know about their financial network?"

"I can't tell you precisely how they invest and store the money. It's a complicated web. Their intelligence unit tracks and manages it all. Real estate, stocks, gold bars, cash, artwork, business investments, off-shore accounts, commercial properties. It's everywhere, and we're going to have a lot of fun untangling it all. But it can be done. They have eight major network centres where the information is stored, and I can tell you the identities of the people who have access. One of the intelligence centres is in Berlin, tucked inside an old bunker system. But I'm sure you already know about that one. We'll need to take care before we go in. What you don't know is that each intelligence facility is wired with detection sensors and enough explosives to wipe out an entire town."

"I want the names of the gatekeepers and blueprints of every facility."

"You'll get all the details when our agreement is made official, signed by your president and the other members of the G20, and only after Kalakia is dead."

"Don't fuck with us on this, Horst," said Burley, his stare hardening, the shadow of the dim light exasperating the harshness of his expression.

"Charles. Language, please," said Stirner. "We need each other. We have to keep our eyes on the prize."

Burley flinched as though an insect had bitten him before reaching into his pocket and taking out his phone. He stared sceptically at the flashing screen before answering.

"Yeah."

He listened carefully for a moment with a neutral expression then hung up.

"Speaking of the prize," said Burley. "He's just appeared on the news show 'Kingdom Come' with Gabby Mechtkempf. He's about to give her an interview. I got to go."

Burley stood up and peered toward his car parked beneath the streetlight while tucking his phone into his pocket.

"An interview?" said Stirner with a sudden high pitch in his voice, giving Burley an incredulous stare. "That can't be true."

"Well, it is. I need to get back. We'll talk later," said Burley and marched off, descending the stairs with two rapid steps then disappearing inside his car before it sped off, leaving a cloud of dust in its wake.

It was a simple yet striking room. Two mustard-coloured armchairs faced each other, with a blue and grey woven carpet beneath. A flat-screen television display was mounted in the corner. In front of Kalakia sat Gabby Mechtkempf, her dark features, angled jaw and sharp, bright gaze giving her a staunch presence. In the background facing the camera was a framed painting depicting a revolutionary fighter planting his flag in the ground as dead bodies lay all around him, while behind him his fellow combatants pointed their rifles toward their enemy. Seeing Mechtkempf in person for the first time, Kalakia decided he had chosen the right person for this moment.

"Hello, viewers," said Mechtkempf to the camera once she was given the signal. "Welcome to 'Kingdom Come.' Joining me today is, and I can't believe I'm saying this…" She looked at Kalakia for a moment before turning back to the camera, blinking multiple times. "Joining me today is… well… Kalakia, the head of The League Of Reckoning."

Kalakia nodded his greeting to Mechtkempf.

"As you all know," began Mechtkempf. "The League Of Reckoning is arguably the best *and* worst kept secret of our generation. Its existence has been felt by all, yet confirmed by very few. Like an invisible hand, wealth inequality has eased considerably over the last decades, with the odd outbreak of violence reminding us that *something* is going on behind the scenes. This harmonic truce between order and chaos, this 'Pax Kalakia' — if I may call it that — has held together since the events of The Worldwide Horror. Now, things have changed. This week's violence has shocked us out of our slumber. The world has pressing questions, and I have the honour of asking them to the man behind it all. As already agreed, Kalakia will allow me to interview him, after which he will have the opportunity to address the audience directly."

There was a pause while Mechtkempf turned from addressing her audience, shuffled her papers, then faced Kalakia.

"Shall we begin?" she said.

"Of course," said Kalakia with a nod.

"So my first question is *why*? Why, after all these years, have you finally decided to reveal your identity?"

Kalakia was sitting back and upright in his armchair, one arm on the rest and the other supporting his head with his index finger pressed against his temple.

"Identity is a fluid concept," he said. "As a reporter who investigates abuses of power, you know this better than most. When power fades, the corrupt person reinvents themselves to regain it. Therefore revealing my identity is not my reason for this interview. I am here because a terrible threat has emerged."

"Which threat?"

"His name is Horst Stirner. He is a former member of my organisation who has betrayed me. The criminal underworld has banded behind him in cooperation with world elites."

"As you already know, the American president gave a speech hours ago on behalf of world leaders declaring the emergence of a so-called 'threat.' What role do our governments have to play in this?"

"Your governments are acting according to what is expedient. They have constituents to please, and a political hierarchy to maintain which relies on the wealthy elites. I have no conflict with your leaders. I understand their predicament. That does not mean I will allow them to fall prey to corrupt forces."

"When the president stated he was going to declare the antagonist in this situation, who do you think he meant?"

"Me, naturally," said Kalakia.

"And is he right? Are you antagonising the world?"

"Ask your viewers if they feel antagonised by me."

"Why did you choose me to speak to?"

"Because you and I share the same values and principles."

"I can hardly espouse violence and murder as part of my value system," said Mechtkempf.

"We merely have different ways of pursuing our values," Kalakia shot back with a cold smirk.

"How deeply have you penetrated our governments?"

"We work with your governments to ensure that wealth is invested back into your hard-working citizens who first helped create it. We do not control or manipulate your governments. They remain an independent entity. If Horst Stirner emerges victorious, that will change."

"But you do control the media, don't you?"

"No," said Kalakia, shaking his head. "We hold some influence in matters of internal security. Although we do alter or quash information which threatens the safety of our people and hinders our work, we do not involve ourselves in the propaganda of your states."

"You mentioned the underworld before as being part of the threat against you. Don't you also have criminals in your organisation?"

"The League Of Reckoning pays no attention to the past indiscretions of its soldiers. Loyalty, tenacity and adherence to our mission are our only concerns."

"I see," said Mechtkempf, pausing for a moment. "What exactly do you do with all the money you confiscate? How do we know we can trust you? And what gives you the right to police the wealthy for money they rightfully earned?"

Kalakia closed his eyes for a moment.

"Thank you, Ms. Mechtkempf," he said. "You ask firm but fair questions. Our work has been well documented. We have provided housing for hundreds of thousands of disenfranchised people. We have forced wages for the working class to consistently increase, and have reinvested wealth to create new opportunities for all. The people have given us this right through their support of us. We get results. Every dollar taken is tracked using a sophisticated software system which must be confirmed in eight different locations before the changes become permanent. Corruption and greed have plagued our organisation in the past, as it does any entity. We keep it at a minimum by enforcing death against those found guilty, all while maintaining a surveillance system of the likes never seen."

"How far does this surveillance system go?"

"That I cannot divulge," said Kalakia.

"And there we have it. What gives you the right to monitor us? Who are you? What's your history, or your track record for that matter? What qualification do you hold for your position?"

"Corruption comes in many guises. It thrives by acting in duplicitous ways, through illusion, manipulation and propaganda. It is never justified. I believe that power must justify its authority at all times. When it can no longer offer a valid reason for its existence, it must be dismantled. I do not claim my position from God. I have no divine right. The leadership is entrusted to me by my people because I have proven myself worthy of it time and again. The results speak for themselves. The minute I falter, the second I cease to be the most capable person for my position, I will gladly stand down. Yet as long as I hold the goodwill of the people, and as long as greed and corruption remain, I will give my life for the cause."

"Don't you think transparency is necessary for power to justify itself, as you put it? Secrecy breeds corruption."

"You are not wrong. Keep in mind that our strength has been in our obscurity. Our enemies could not strike out against a foe they could not see. The shadow is a fertile source of power."

"And now you have stepped out of the shadow because…?"

"Our enemy struck from within, not from without."

"I see. That brings me to the next question, one which has been on everyone's lips since a video of him in a fistfight in London went viral. Who is this young man?"

The television screen displayed a photo of Frederich on a backdrop of a screaming crowd, his flying fist suspended in the air as the colossal Dikka's head flew back in a bloody mess. The grim determination on Frederich's face along with his fluttering brown locks looked iconic.

When Kalakia had first seen the picture, he immediately recalled the story of David and Goliath. The reality was not so clear cut, but that was not important. The photo would tell whatever tale the people needed to hear. In their state of fear they would relate to the small and vulnerable 'David,' with Frederich's Goliath-like opponent representing the shadow of destruction hanging over them. Kalakia and Mechtkempf had discussed the matter of Frederich before going on air, and she had wanted to confirm if Kalakia was fine with her mentioning the talented Estonian in the segment. Kalakia thought long and hard, and decided that the risk was worth it. To win over the populace, he would need to present them their hero. In much the same way that Fidel

Castro had ridden into Havana on the back of Che Guevara's revolutionary fervour, Kalakia knew that Frederich's zeal and savagery would provide him the upper-hand in the upcoming propaganda battle.

"His name is Frederich Abel," said Kalakia. "And he is an orphan. He has no family and no fear. His life has one purpose and one alone; justice for the people."

"Footage was released only hours ago by the Polish authorities revealing him to be the person who killed the Berlin Bomber," said Mechtkempf. "Can you confirm this to be true?"

"Yes," said Kalakia. "He witnessed the carnage of the bombing with his own eyes, and took it upon himself to bring retribution upon the terrorists."

"The authorities and witnesses said they were sickened by what they saw. How can you approve of such brutal methods?"

"It is easy to judge his acts from a distance. The demonic forces of this world do not compromise or negotiate. Evil bows only to fear, and it has a reason to fear this man. He is a force of nature never before seen. He does what needs to be done. However, the people can rest assured knowing that he is on their side. He fights for you."

"Why?" said Mechtkempf.

"He knows no other way. His past made him savage, but his suffering has made him sympathetic to the pain of the people. He understands their plight."

"Thank you," said Mechtkempf with the slightest of smiles. "Those are all the questions I had. I believe you would now like to address our audience directly?"

The cameraman moved around to face Kalakia head-on, and Kalakia turned away from Mechtkempf and looked into the lens. After a moment, the cameraman signalled with his finger that Kalakia could begin.

"Fellow citizens," said Kalakia. "I come to you today representing the organisation responsible for the equality you have enjoyed for decades. Since our inception, our mission has been to bring justice to those disparaged by the corrupt. We have indeed achieved this end by acting with impunity, and in the process, have committed many violent acts. Our success lies not in our brutality, however, but in our principles. Not once have we pursued recognition or glory, not once have we targeted the civilian population except with due cause. During our reign, inequality has been reduced to levels never before seen in history. You know this because you have reaped the benefits. Where economic hardship has reared its ugly head, we have worked with your governments to ensure ongoing prosperity for the disenfranchised, without bowing to your wealthy elites. It is no secret that once a certain amount of wealth is achieved, a person ceases to identify with the common man. They become a different species, cold and calculating, unbound by shame and unhinged in their capacity for greed and destruction. Their thirst for power is unquenchable — until they meet their reckoning. Popular backing for our global hegemony of justice remains, which is the reason your governments have thus far supported the status quo.

"This era of prosperity for the common person is now under threat. Firstly, those few who have not benefited from our doctrine, namely the greedy and corrupt, have struck back. Like rabid dogs, their frustration has come to a head, and they have assembled behind the man who promised them the key to my organisation; Horst Stirner. It is they who have sown the recent chaos, and who seek to upend

232

The League Of Reckoning. If you, the people, accept the lie which you will be told tomorrow, then you will have granted permission for tyranny to reinstate itself. I will be the first to admit of our evil nature, yet without us, true evil in this world would multiply beyond imagination.

"I have thus far resisted the attempts of the greedy and corrupt to reveal my identity. I do not answer to them, nor will I ever. Rather, it is my honour to come now before you, the people, to implore you to fight. Let your governments hear your might roar. Take to the streets, raise your voices, rise as free people, and declare your demand for justice and freedom from tyranny. Legitimacy and authority shall never come from above, but from us, the people. Support me, and I promise you; Horst Stirner will meet my wrath, as will his band of traitors and criminals."

Kalakia leaned further forward and clenched his fist, presenting it to the camera.

"Do not forget," he said. "We are the people, and *we* are the power. "

26

Frederich could not understand the conversation between Camille and the policeman, but he did not need to know French to grasp what was being said. The tone of their voices gave him a general idea:

"How long is this bastard going to stay like this?"

"As long as it takes. He still has an infection."

"An infection shouldn't last this long!"

"Oh? I should know how long an infection lasts."

"He can sleep in his prison cell."

"Don't you give me that. Let me do my job and stop interfering."

The conversation ended abruptly with what sounded like a barrage of insults from the policeman before he marched out and slammed the door behind him. Frederich waited some seconds after the room grew silent before opening one eye slightly, then the other. Camille was standing in the middle of the room rubbing her temples. She exhaled and looked out of the window.

"You can't keep this up forever," said Frederich with a low voice.

"I know," said Camille, going over to sit on the chair beside Frederich's bed. "Two more days. I hope they will come to their senses."

Not a chance, thought Frederich, expecting a beatdown as soon as they got their hands on him.

"I can handle myself, you know," he said.

"I am sure," said Camille. "Two more days. Then you can face the law."

"I still don't understand why you're doing this," said Frederich.

"I don't need you to understand," replied Camille.

"I've faced worse things than some hero cop."

Camille sharpened her gaze, paying close attention to Frederich's face.

"What kinds of things?" she asked.

Psychopaths. Sadists. Murderers. You name it.

"Just more dangerous people," he said with a shrug.

"How did you get the scars on your back?" she asked. "I saw them when I was operating on your leg."

The bear from his dream came up, towering above his tiny frame, and he blinked hard. He saw *her* eyes again, glowing with terror that oozed beneath his skin. He knew who she was, but could not bring himself to say it. He preferred not to go there. It was easier that way. No need to dwell on it. He also recalled his hallucination with the bear while he was locked up in Scheffler's hole. Every time he saw the scars in the mirror, after a shower or while getting changed, he simply glossed over them. They stopped existing after a while. He was only reminded of them when people asked.

"It happened when I was a kid," he said.

"They look strange. Not from a knife. Was it an animal?"

He nodded.

"A bear," he said.

"I see," said Camille with a tone of awe, her eyes glowing and lips parting. "How old were you?"

236

"Six or seven."

"Where were your parents?"

He saw *her* again, crawling over the dirt, her terror singeing into his being. A pulse of rage shot up, and his entire body shook. *Stay out.* Every one of his muscles tensed up, almost cutting off his breathing.

Camille read him carefully, then nodded.

"It's ok," she said gently. "It's fine. It's fine."

Frederich sniffed and looked away, sensing the episode pass and his body grow somewhat calm again.

The door suddenly burst open. The policeman marched in, scowling, his moustached-face bright red. He pointed accusingly at Frederich and began screaming in French, moving gradually closer until Camille rose up from her chair and tried to hold him back. The confrontation quickly escalated into a scrum, Camille's pure white doctor's uniform facing off against the policeman's navy blue authority. Camille once again proved her tenacity, holding her own against the fury of the unhinged officer. He progressed forward, pointing, pushing and yelling, while Camille dug in her heels and pressed firmly against his chest, resisting not just with her body but her words. Frederich's leg throbbed as he sat up in a state of vigilance, ready for a fight in case the man broke through Camille's defences. He looked around for a weapon but only saw a small metal tray on the side table with an empty plastic cup on it. The screaming grew louder, the struggle turning more frantic, before the policeman won out. Camille was pushed suddenly to the side, managing to keep her feet, but too slow to recover to catch the police officer. Frederich braced himself as the man came toward him and tried to grasp his shoulder, to which he deflected the man's arm to the side. The officer continued to be frustrated in his attempts to get a hold of Frederich before suddenly reverting to punches. Frederich lifted his elbow and blocked a fist aimed at his head, while pain shot out of his leg again from the sudden movements and contractions. He groaned out loud when the policeman landed a hard punch in his stomach.

It was enough to force him out of his defensive posture. He reached to the side and grasped the metal tray, slamming it over the policeman's head. The officer went tumbling backwards, the rage in his bulging eyes intense enough for Frederich to anticipate the worst. It came when he took his gun out of its holster. Frederich had a split second to act. He lunged at the man with all his might and landed on top of him, softening his fall somewhat. The impact on his leg was too much. He yelled out like a madman, the pain so great that he went out of his mind. When his focus returned, the policeman was on top of him with his fingers around Frederich's throat. As Frederich struggled to draw oxygen, *it* came rushing up, obliterating any sense of reason Frederich was holding onto. At that moment, Camille came from behind and tried to pull the man off. Her sudden appearance caused the policeman's grip to loosen, and Frederich saw his opening. He slapped the man's arms to the side, lifted his torso and punched him in the throat. The man rolled over and grasped his neck while yelling in pain. Frederich quickly sat up and rolled over, hot in the face and panting hard. There was room for nothing else; he wanted to slaughter the bastard. The metal tray was sitting at his side with a dint in the middle. He picked it up and brought it down hard on top of the policeman's head. Then again. His entire body was on fire. It had consumed him, compelling him to beat his foe to a pulp.

"Stop it!" yelled Camille when Frederich was preparing to land a third blow. "Don't kill him!"

The intensity in her voice caused Frederich to turn his head automatically. He caught her eyes, which were begging him to stop. He remained frozen with his arms raised, trembling all over. The accumulated energy in his body was immense. The feeling it gave him was infernal, its instruction was clear; *kill that son of a bitch!*

"No," said Camille, shaking her head. "Don't do it. I beg you."

The vigour in her eyes drew him in, and was compelling enough to draw him away from the inferno inside. The pressure in his head eased. The policeman's groans found their way to his consciousness. Feeling came back to his shoulders and arms, and then to his stomach and legs. Tears filled his eyes as he thawed. The rage eased back to its source. He lowered the tray and looked down at the barely conscious policeman, who had blood running down his entire face. Camille approached and cautiously reached out and took hold of Frederich's weapon. Frederich held it tight for a moment, then released his grip. Camille carefully placed the piece of metal on the ground then kneeled beside him and the policeman.

"It's fine," she said, speaking softly. "Let me look at him."

Frederich inhaled deeply as he reacquainted himself with his body, then wiped the tears from his eyes. He flipped over, grunting from the pain in his leg. Camille turned to the police officer and placed her ear next to his mouth. She then stood up and went over to the door and opened it. Frederich could hear her steps disappearing down the hallway. Moments later she came back with another doctor, a bright-eyed, dark-skinned woman in her twenties, who looked down at the scene with shocked fascination. Camille said something to her in French, and the doctor went to tend to the police officer. Camille returned to Frederich's side and began inspecting his leg.

"Are you ok?" she asked.

Frederich nodded while in a daze. By now he had numbed out the pain; the light-headedness, the adrenaline and the throbbing blending together into a cohesive, dissociative state. So when the two burly men suddenly appeared at the door, they looked like merchants of death, dressed in all-black from head to toe and their faces cold and stiff. Frederich could do nothing, only gaze up at them helplessly. The men calmly inspected the scene before turning their attention to Frederich.

"Abel," said one of the men. "Scheffler sent us. Let's go."

The man bent down and grasped Frederich's wrist, but Camille intercepted him.

"Leave him alone," she ordered.

The soldier responded by reaching into his jacket pocket.

"No," said Frederich to the man before turning to Camille. "They're with me. If you don't let them take me, they'll kill you."

Camille understood immediately. Whatever fight she still had immediately dispersed, and she frowned and lowered her head. She retreated backwards, appearing aged and pale. The soldier did not waste time, grasping Frederich by the armpits and lifting him with one smooth motion. The other soldier stepped forward and the two men used their shoulders to support him with each arm.

Frederich gazed at the weary Camille, who was now sitting on the floor. Too much had happened for him to know what to say. Something significant in him had shifted; he knew that much. He managed to conjure a weak smile and nodded his thanks to the unrelenting woman who had bravely fought to save his life. Camille blinked several times but did not respond. Using his one good leg for support, Frederich let the soldiers drag him forward as they walked out in unison and crossed the hallway. They pushed the glass door open and received a shocked stare from the man at reception as they continued toward the elevator. The receptionist looked on for a time before half-heartedly yelling something out. The elevator door slid open and they got in. On the ground level they received more stares from those in the waiting area.

Outside Frederich savoured the fresh air on his face while the three of them headed together to the carpark. Frederich raised his chin and paid close attention. In the distance was what sounded like the chanting of a crowd. The soldiers said nothing, only placing Frederich on the back seat of their black Mercedes with his back to the door and his wounded leg stretched across. They drove off in silence, and had barely left the hospital grounds when they were forced to stop. Frederich watched on curiously through the windshield at the enormous wall of people clogging the street ahead. The crowd marched by with no sign of their numbers dwindling. The soldier who was driving mumbled something to himself then did a U-turn. At the next main intersection they stopped again. There were more marchers. Some of them had their fists raised in the air.

"What's going on?" said Frederich finally.

Neither of the soldiers responded. Frederich rolled his window down and tried to pick out what they were chanting. It sounded like they were repeating the word 'kamaka.' *Kamaka?* He focussed harder. Then his skin crawled. It was not 'kamaka' that they were chanting. They were yelling 'Kalakia.'

The car suddenly jerked forward and turned right, racing toward the next intersection, where there were yet more marchers. This time Frederich and his two companions were forced to stop for good. They had nowhere else to go except back to the hospital. Frederich looked out at the scene and his eyeballs almost popped out of their sockets. His attention was drawn to a sign being held up by one of the protestors with a picture on it. He lost all feeling in his face and his mouth gradually fell open. He stopped breathing, mesmerised by what he was seeing. He recognised the crowd from the Stern and Dolly, as well as Dikka, who in the picture was falling backwards. The guy landing the punch looked foreign to Frederich, even though he was one-hundred-percent certain that it was him. The man in the photo looked heroic, like someone worthy of having their name chanted by thousands of people. So why were they shouting Frederich's name?

"Abel! Abel! Abel!" came their collective voices, each yell of his name sending a wave of goosebumps though his entire body. *Have they lost their minds?* Their march continued on, before another blown-up poster of the strange hero figure appeared, accompanied by more chants of Frederich's name, as Frederich felt whatever identity he possessed being slowly devoured by the crowd.

27

The streetlights along Mohammed VI Avenue looked like stars from where Kalakia was standing, while the headlights of the vehicles passing through the esplanade were like shooting stars. The smell of salt wafted up from the water, which gurgled and whooshed along the side of the yacht. It was a typical evening in Tangier, the air warm and thick, the pace steady and undisturbed. The gateway city from the Atlantic Ocean to the Mediterranean had so far resisted the worldwide chaos which gripped the globe since Kalakia's call to arms.

"There's no sign of the demonstrations letting up," said Francois, approaching from behind. "Moscow, Beijing and London have tried police crackdowns and failed. There are just too many people. No sign of an official response either. We should get the call soon."

Kalakia checked the time. The cancelled G20 meeting was meant to take place hours ago. The sheer pressure of the demonstrations would have leaders scrambling to walk back their new relationship with Stirner while trying to save face. Kalakia felt no pity for them.

"Where are they?" he said.

"They're in the air and should be here soon. Tamju Lau and Marco Lessio were held up by demonstrations."

Kalakia nodded, and Francois returned to the enclosed upper-deck area which Kalakia could not stomach being in. It was his churning stomach and restless legs which had brought him outside.

He had hoped to delay this moment for as long as possible; indefinitely if he had his way. It was Stirner who changed the rules. He had tried the oldest trick in the power playbook; instigate chaos and round up the terrified sheep into his paddock. That left Kalakia no other choice. He had to go all in. He could do so because he had the better hand; he knew his grassroots support was too strong, that when push came to shove the public would choose him. Stirner's idealism had faced off against Kalakia's Realpolitik, and it had lost. Everyone would feel the consequences. Global power had been unmoored, and it brought Kalakia no pleasure to witness it consolidate beneath his banner in every major city. There were no victors in such situations. It was merely the lesser of two evils, with Stirner being the greater. Now the fate of the world had been irreversibly altered. Where it went from there, not even Kalakia could predict. The likelihood of returning to the status quo was slim to none. Recent events had accelerated the globalisation process and shattered trust in government. The potential for revolution or civil war would loom in the mind of every leader and citizen.

Kalakia was feeling the pressure to embrace the role of global demagogue. News channels from all around the world showed masses of people of every race chanting his name. The League had become the dominant topic on social media. The thought of a media circus centred around him made him nauseous. He continued ruminating and pacing restlessly along the edge of the yacht for some time before the helicopter carrying his Generals came buzzing in the distance.

Scheffler stared out of the window as their chopper cruised along the beachside above the Tangier city lights before turning toward Kalakia's yacht. The vessel grew gradually in size as the pilot descended on approach, the enormous 'H' on the landing pad drawing closer until it was all Scheffler could see. Then with the tiniest of bumps, they had safely touched down. Scheffler forced the door open and lowered his head before jumping out, followed by Marco Lessio and Daps Limbaba. Tamju Lau remained inside for some time longer, calmly rising from his seat and disembarking with careful steps. The four men moved under cover before the helicopter lifted and disappeared over the sea, back in the direction it came.

Once the droning had faded, Kalakia appeared from around the corner and walked toward his Generals. The five men stood silently for a long time in a state of heightened tension, until Kalakia moved to open the door to the upper-deck cabin. He held it in place while Lau, Lessio and Limbaba entered the luxurious space, each of them giving him a firm look on their way in. Scheffler paused before following, first glancing nervously at the fast disappearing coastline as the yacht headed toward the open Atlantic.

The interior was what Scheffler expected from a luxury yacht. The gigantic space had a loaded bar, enough leather-seating to hold a decent congregation and a round meeting table with leather chairs. Beneath his feet were timber floorboards and above were two chandeliers surrounded by a series of downlights scattered in a suspended ceiling. He joined the others at the meeting table, followed by Kalakia, who closed the door behind him and took his seat.

"This was your plan the whole time?" said Lessio immediately. "You should have warned us, dammit!"

Kalakia stared blankly at him.

"This is exactly what happened to The Council," said Limbaba, shaking his head. "Do you not trust us, Kalakia? Are we expendable, like them?"

"You are walking down a dangerous path," said Tamju Lau. "And you are taking us all with you."

The Generals' frustrations had festered for the entirety of the tense helicopter ride. Kalakia had startled the organisation with his latest stunt, acting with unprecedented impunity. As Generals, the four men could not tolerate such blatant disrespect. It was not passivity that had brought them this far. They lived in a kill or be killed world. It was into this world that they had now released their resentment, which hung thick over the table while the Generals cautiously awaited Kalakia's reaction.

The table remained motionless. The Generals knew they had lashed out against a man who ordered people killed for far less. They remained frozen between the opposing pressure of their exasperation and their fear of their leader.

Kalakia looked at each of them one by one. When his stare met with Scheffler's, his pupils looked terrifying, having expanded enough to fill his eyes. Fear shot through Scheffler's heart, causing his jaw to tense and his body to lift off the chair. He scanned the area briefly and realised that he had not seen any members of Supreme Force on arrival. Kalakia's protectors had not left his side once since Stirner's betrayal. Was this it? Were they hiding, ready to storm the room and terminate the Four Generals the same way as their predecessors?

"You question my authority?" said Kalakia with a low voice, maintaining eye contact with Scheffler.

"We…" began Scheffler, his throat thick and lumpy. He was having difficulty drawing air, expecting a violent outburst at any second.

"I did not reveal my plan because you were unworthy of it," said Kalakia, not waiting for Scheffler to complete his sentence. "And I shall tell you why. Each of you had an opportunity at the council of war to demonstrate your wisdom and insight, but only your lack of imagination showed."

Scheffler shuffled in his chair while Kalakia turned his attention toward Tamju Lau.

"Tamju, you rightly stressed caution, but did not provide a path forward. Your scepticism cripples you. It must be tempered with decisive action." Kalakia turned directly to Marco Lessio. "Your hunger for conflict continues to blind you. So far I have seen no sign of the cunning man whose wit drives his enemies mad, and whose love for his men earns their unquestioned loyalty. How carelessly you sent them into battle without a second thought." Lessio's face blushed as he bit his lower lip and looked away, while Kalakia shifted his focus to Daps Limbaba. "Daps, your loyalty and strength are powerful assets, but you continue to crave an outer voice to direct you. I know that you grieve your father, but you must let him die once and for all. Slaughter him, and feast on his remains, so that you may become him. His wisdom lives on inside you, but only if you dare to claim it. Or do you not trust yourself?"

Limbaba's eyes watered up at the mention of his father, meanwhile Scheffler already knew what Kalakia was going to

247

tell him. He looked down at the table to escape his leader's all-seeing eye.

"Vincent," said Kalakia, waiting for Scheffler to look up at him. "You have impressed me of late, but your self-doubt and impatience continue to sabotage you. Be mindful of them, and remember what I told you."

Scheffler frowned and nodded. Kalakia looked over each of his Generals again one by one.

"You want respect?" he said, now raising his voice. "Earn it! Do not come to me with your wounded egos. Your position does not guarantee you your rights — you must earn those rights by proving yourselves worthy of your position. I acted alone because thus far not one of you has proven his capability at this level."

A deep sense of shame washed over Scheffler, forcing his head to drop. Looking around, he noticed that Kalakia's harsh yet magnanimous words had surgically and thoroughly deflated all of the Generals.

"You are here because you are the best," continued Kalakia. "I hope you will put aside such pettiness and rise to meet the upcoming challenges we will be facing."

The table remained silent for a long time. Each person escaped into their own mind, their stares vacant and contemplative. Kalakia said nothing further, as though daring someone else to step up and speak. Scheffler cleared his throat.

"We're ready for anything," he said. "The soldiers are laying low for the time being. There's not much anyone can do until the mayhem dies down."

"Of course," said Kalakia. "We are in unprecedented territory."

"That's an understatement," said Scheffler.

"We've got to focus on finding Stirner," said Marco Lessio, signalling his re-engagement. "He's the key, right?"

"Right," said Scheffler. "We spotted Vidrik while he was leaving Paris, but we lost him once the crowds began to gather. We're scanning the area, in case he shows up. I've got a feeling he can lead us to Stirner."

"Vidrik knows our intelligence network well," said Kalakia. "It is no coincidence that you lost him."

"Well, here's hoping he slips up."

"What about Frederich?" said Kalakia. "Clearly he failed in his pursuit of Vidrik."

"He caught a gunshot from the police. Our soldiers just picked him up from the hospital."

"Is it serious?" said Kalakia, leaning forward.

"No. It's a leg wound, went straight through without touching any bones or nerves. He's young. He'll be fine."

"Where is he now?" said Kalakia.

"On the way to Berlin. He'll need to rest that leg for a little while."

"Is he fit to speak?"

"Are you kidding? Even with one leg, he got into a dust-up with a policeman in the hospital and almost killed him. I think he's fine."

Kalakia relaxed back into his chair.

"Not sure he's happy about being thrown into the spotlight like that though," added Scheffler.

"His situation is of his own making," said Kalakia. "His idolisation by the masses is a consequence of his reckless actions."

"Fair point," said Scheffler. "Nobody told him to walk into a London pub and start a brawl in front of fifty people."

"His face is now recognisable all over the world," said Tamju Lau. "How will he do his job?"

The table fell silent. It was a good question.

"He will need to become one with the darkness," Limbaba said finally. "You say he is wounded?"

"Yeah," said Scheffler.

"Don't take him to Berlin," said Limbaba. "He needs more than rest. He is the people's hero, but he is far too troubled to meet their expectations. He is not ready for what lies ahead. I propose we take him to the witch doctor of my hometown. His name is Fourtani. He can help the boy heal his body and spirit, and he can show him how to blend into the night."

"People still believe in that shit?" said Marco Lessio.

Limbaba shrugged.

"I don't understand it, but it works. I send my soldiers to Fourtani when I see them in distress, and he heals them every time."

"What do you think?" said Scheffler, looking at Kalakia.

"Do it," said Kalakia. "Nothing else has succeeded."

"Fine," said Scheffler. "I'll have him flown out asap."

When the matter seemed settled, Tamju Lau leaned forward and steepled his hands.

"We must move quickly," he said. "With chaos comes opportunity."

"Correct," said Kalakia. "Our window is short, and we must act while we have the backing of the people. Stirner is cornered. He will be at his most dangerous now. We must strike hard. We must hunt him and his people down, and we must kill them all."

"I guess the time for misdirection is over then?" said Scheffler.

"Now is the time to bring down the hammer," said Kalakia with a tiny smirk.

Scheffler smiled and nodded.

"So let's talk strategy," said Marco Lessio, shuffling around in his chair to prepare for the night-long discussion. "I've got a few ideas."

Brunswick was jolted from her sleep, waking up to the pitch black of her room.

She oriented herself in a state of numbness. All she could hear in the dark was her heart beating. Her lips were dry, and her nose felt stuffy. *Damn hay fever season.* She felt the urge to go to the bathroom, and reached over and switched on her lamp. She almost screamed when she saw Stirner standing beside her bed looking down at her.

"God!" she squealed, falling back and lifting her hands defensively.

Stirner looked like death. He towered above her with no sign of his pretend charm. His squint was gone, and pursed lips had replaced his ugly smirk. The severity in his wide-open eyes alarmed Brunswick.

"What's going on?" she asked.

Stirner did not move, only remained staring at her. She prepared to defend herself, sure now that he would lash out with a concealed weapon. There was a glass of water on her side table which she could toss at his head. Should she make the first move? Or wait for him to strike first? She stood by, carefully watching his eyes for clues. There was nobody there. They looked grave and lifeless.

"You have a deal," said Stirner suddenly. "Secure the nuclear missiles, and you'll have everything you asked for."

Stirner then turned around and left the room. Brunswick remained frozen for a long time before rolling onto her back and looking up at the ceiling. Only then did she remember to breathe again.

The slow, thumping beat of Manowar's 'Warriors of the World' instantly lifted Vidrik's spirits. He turned the volume knob on the stereo to the maximum and stood nodding to the beat with his eyes closed. In the spirit of an archetypal Manowar album illustration, he pictured himself standing atop a fiery mountain of rubble and corpses, gloriously raising Frederich Abel's severed head to the sky while Ida lay naked at his feet, holding up his victory crown. The image brought him incalculable pleasure. *If only.*

He picked up the photo of Ida from the cocktail party and lay back on his bed, studying every inch of her. For a moment he grieved the loss of her innocence while his chest ached. He longed for the starry-eyed, ignorant little girl.

She was gone now. In her place was the new Ida; a goddess yearning to be fucked. Only it was clear by that little scuffle of theirs that he would need to earn the right. He knew from the countless whores he had left in his wake that a *real* woman did not come easily. And what a fight she had put up! Vidrik had no idea she had it in her. What a shame she had to push him over the edge like that. It was unnecessary. No one desired her like Vidrik. She had to know that. Vidrik would bet his life that nobody had ever seen her the way he did. Not even Abel. *Especially* not an inexperienced little boy like Abel.

As Vidrik began to focus more on his nemesis, the music reached its crescendo. The electric guitar was buzzing with the intensity of a formula-one car, and the beat was unrelenting. Vidrik felt his inner warrior come alive and consume him like fire. Manowar always did that for him. Although Abel had interrupted Vidrik's quality time with Ida, Vidrik knew the last laugh had been his. That little game of cat and mouse through the streets of Paris had been fun. It had also revealed Abel's weakness; his pathetic, predictable, overflowing pride.

Vidrik could not have planned a better ending to their game. He was amazed to see Abel go down with a gunshot wound, relieved that it had only struck his leg. Abel, killed by police? How dreadful. No, Abel's life belonged to him, and only him. Just like nobody would get in the way of him and Ida, nothing would stop him from claiming Abel's life. And who knew? Maybe when he finally had his man, he would still decide to cut off his ugly head and hold it to the sky, just like a warrior should when he vanquishes his enemy.

CPSIA information can be obtained
at www.ICGtesting.com
Printed in the USA
LVHW040932181119
637663LV00006B/2424